A FALL FOR FRIENDSHIP

Don't miss the place where
the adventures began!

ICE CREAM SUMMER
ONCE UPON A WINTER

Or the adventures to come!

A SPRING TO REMEMBER

AN ORCHARD NOVEL

A FALL FOR FRIENDSHIP

By Megan Atwood

Illustrated by Natalie Andrewson

ALADDIN

New York London Toronto Sydney New Delhi

ALADDIN

An imprint of Simon & Schuster Children's Publishing Division

1230 Avenue of the Americas, New York, New York 10020

First Aladdin hardcover edition September 2018

Text copyright © 2018 by Simon & Schuster, Inc.

Illustrations copyright © 2018 by Natalie Andrewson

All rights reserved, including the right of reproduction in whole or in part in any form.

ALADDIN and related logo are registered trademarks of Simon & Schuster, Inc.

For information about special discounts for bulk purchases, please contact Simon & Schuster Special Sales at 1-866-506-1949 or business@simonandschuster.com.

The Simon & Schuster Speakers Bureau can bring authors to your live event. For more information or to book an event contact the Simon & Schuster Speakers Bureau at 1-866-248-3049 or visit our website at www.simonspeakers.com.

Book designed by Laura Lyn DiSiena

The illustrations for this book were rendered digitally.

The text of this book was set in Baskerville.

Manufactured in the United States of America 0818 FFG

10 9 8 7 6 5 4 3 2 1

Library of Congress Cataloging-in-Publication Data

Names: Atwood, Megan, author. | Andrewson, Natalie, illustrator.

Title: A fall for friendship / by Megan Atwood ; illustrated by Natalie Andrewson.

Description: First Aladdin hardcover edition. | New York : Aladdin, [2018] | Series: An Orchard novel ; 3 | Summary: "Olive doesn't believe in ghosts, but she does admit something weird is going on at the orchard"—Provided by publisher.

Identifiers: LCCN 2017057975 |

ISBN 9781481490511 (hc) | ISBN 9781481490528 (eBook)

Subjects: | CYAC: Friendship—Fiction. | Ghosts—Fiction. |

Halloween—Fiction. | Apples—Fiction. | Orchards—Fiction. |

New England—Fiction. | Humorous stories.

Classification: LCC PZ7.A8952 Fal 2018 | DDC [Fic]—dc23

LC record available at https://lccn.loc.gov/2017057975

For my mother, who gave me life and a love for words: Malola Atwood.

CHAPTER 1
But ... Is It REAL?

Actually, no Halloween monsters REALLY exist," Olive said, pushing up her glasses, then reaching over for more apple pie. "Zombies are a great example," she went on. "Scientifically, zombies aren't physically possible." She piled her plate high with the pie and then added some ice cream. It wasn't until she'd finished that she saw the whole table looking at her.

Her dad John beamed, but her other dad,

David, smiled and looked down, shaking his head a little. Lizzie's parents—Albert and Tabitha Garrison—shared a smile too. But Olive's twin brother, Peter, and their friends Lizzie and Sarah all just looked exasperated.

"You don't know for sure, Olive. There might be one somewhere in the world," Sarah said, spooning a big cloud of whipped cream onto her pie. "Anyway, we're talking about the zombie hayride, not REAL zombies."

Olive furrowed her eyebrows. "Yeah. Because there's no such thing as 'real' zombies." She wasn't sure why Sarah wasn't listening to her. Sure, zombies were something she and her brother had been obsessed with for years. . . . And when they'd moved to New Amity and met Lizzie and Sarah, they'd found out they loved zombies too.

AND they all got to plan a zombie hayride for a fall activity at the Garrison Orchard—not to mention a haunted barn. But that didn't make zombies *real*. Surely Sarah knew that?

Lizzie continued the conversation, clearing her throat. "So, for the hayride, we can put an ad up around New Amity for people who want to be zombies. We'll have to tell them that they'll probably be hit by Nerf darts. And then Gloria and her friends will be the actors in the haunted barn."

"ACTING!" Gloria, Lizzie's teenage sister, yelled at the end of the table. Her sunglasses slipped a little down her nose as she threw her arms out, but she pushed them up and went back to reading a book called *Acting the Strange and Unusual*. Olive was used to Gloria yelling "Acting!" whenever anyone mentioned, well, acting.

Her dad David called Gloria a "free spirit."

A smile broke out over Lizzie's face—a smile that Olive couldn't help returning, even if she was still kind of smarting from Sarah's irritation with her. Lizzie's smiles were always contagious. Plus, Olive was super-excited about the festivities. This was the first year the Garrison Orchard would be putting on the zombie hayride and the haunted barn. And she, Peter, Lizzie, and Sarah were right in the thick of it.

It wasn't just the four friends who were excited, either. The hayride and the haunted barn were the talk of everyone in their school. Kids were betting each other they wouldn't go in, and Olive had even seen two kids crying because they were scared even at the mention of it. She thought that was silly. What was there to be scared of? It was just a bunch of kids Gloria's age acting. None of it was real. Now, river parasites? THOSE were real. And something to be afraid of.

Albert said to Gloria, "Honey, why don't you go over what you and your friends have planned?"

Gloria looked up from her book and pulled down her glasses. Then she pushed them back up her nose and sniffed. "Very well. If you insist," she said, setting the book down. She put both hands on the table and leaned in, her voice dark and ominous. "First, the victims—"

Tabitha interrupted, "The paying guests," but Gloria barely paused.

She went on, "—the victims will enter the barn, where darkness will envelop them. A monster greets them, his fangs dripping with blood. 'Welcome, my delicious dinner—I mean, guests,' he will say, and

5

beckon them to follow him." Olive couldn't help it, she leaned in a little. "From there, the victims will feel their way around the barn, all the while being chased by ghosts, by vampires, by creatures of the night bent on their destruction! The first scene they come upon: a circus! Monstrous clowns ask them to come play, their smiles unnatural, their eyes wild—"

And suddenly, Lizzie cut in, something she never did. In fact, Lizzie wasn't usually a talker, but this whole night she'd been animated and gabby. Sarah hadn't even had to translate most of her sentences. Lizzie said, "Yes! The first room is the clown room! Then it's the werewolf room, where a moon turns full and the actor turns into a wolf. Meanwhile, the zombies from the hay-ride will come through—or at least that's what the guests will think—and start following them.

The next room will be a chainsaw murderer, and then there's a ghost school where bloody kids will answer questions about haunting, and then—"

Gloria huffed loudly. "BABIES need to wait their turns," she said, and slammed herself backward against her chair. Lizzie's face turned immediately regretful.

"Oh, no. I interrupted you, didn't I?" she said, her eyes worried and scrunched. Sarah patted her shoulder. Gloria ignored her and put her headphones on, apparently done with the story.

Sarah shrugged and went on, "Anyway, after the haunting rooms, it's a scary dentist room, and then people walk by the hayloft and it ends with a—"

And here Lizzie interrupted again, "—with a real murder scene! Or, not real, really, of course. But we're going to have some actors up in the loft arguing, and then one of them is going to push the other one off. She'll fall into some soft hay, but the audience won't see the hay. And when she gets up, she'll be like a ghost who will chase everyone out of the barn!" Lizzie made a squealing noise again and bounced in her chair. Sarah bounced too. Peter grinned. Lizzie ended with, "It won't be a real ghost, of course."

Olive laughed. "Well, yeah . . . because there's no such thing as a real ghost. . . ." But she noticed no one else was laughing. In fact, they looked a little annoyed with *her*.

"What?" she said.

Sarah huffed. "You don't KNOW there's no such thing," she said.

Before Olive could answer, Peter said, "It sounds awesome, Lizzie. We are all so excited."

Lizzie beamed. Peter threw Olive a look.

This time, Olive didn't smile back. Why weren't her friends listening to her? And why did they insist on saying things were real, when they KNEW they weren't? Suddenly, she felt like one of the grown-ups instead of one of her friends.

Tabitha smiled at all of them. "Why don't you all come tomorrow morning and help with the setup? Most of the town will be here to help, and you can ask them to put up flyers there. And maybe even finagle some volunteers!"

"DEAL!" yelled Sarah. She high-fived Lizzie on one side of her. And then Peter on the other. But she didn't high-five Olive on the other side of Peter.

Olive wanted to believe that she didn't because she was too far away. But she had a feeling she was making that up.

CHAPTER 2
The Curse of the Clumsy

Peter looked thoughtful. Which was kind of the way Peter always looked. But this time, he was thoughtful about something he wanted to say to Olive. She could tell. And Olive was growing impatient.

John and David walked up ahead, holding hands and pointing things out on their walk to the Garrisons' barn. The place was a fair walk away, but their dads were charmed by the fall weather. And even though Olive was definitely chilly, she too loved the zip in the air and the crunch of the leaves.

She didn't love the weighty silence, though. "What?" she finally asked Peter. He had grabbed her arm to let their dads get ahead so they could talk. Which was what normally happened. After all, they were twins; they always talked to each other. But the minute she'd seen his face, she'd known it wasn't going to be a conversation where they joked around.

"Maybe you could . . . I don't know. Lay off the whole 'things aren't real' thing," he said, looking ahead.

Olive laughed. "But . . . zombies *aren't* real. And neither are ghosts."

Peter shrugged, and now Olive stopped in the middle of the road. "You don't *really* believe in those sorts of things, do you?" Her voice was louder than she meant it to be. Their dads glanced back, and Peter gave her a "keep your voice down" look.

"I don't know. I'm not saying they're real. I'm saying I don't know. I've had some interesting things happen to me, that's all. Things that didn't have a logical explanation. Maybe you can keep an open mind," he said.

"But you're asking me to pretend that something is real when it's not! That's not . . ." She wasn't exactly sure what she wanted to say. Just that she felt like her shirt was on too tight. Or her coat was too far up her neck. Like all of a sudden things didn't feel right. She felt like he was asking her to fit into something she didn't fit into.

"I'm not, Olive. I'm asking you to let your friends believe what they want to believe. And to maybe think that you don't know everything in the world," Peter said. He walked faster, and Olive could tell he was mad. He moved ahead of her.

Turning around, he said, "Why is it so important to you that we all believe the same thing?" He kicked an acorn and watched it bounce to the side of the road.

Olive sighed and stuck her hands in her pockets, watching her feet walk along the gravel road. She didn't know exactly why it was important to her. But it was. Really important. Because she cared about the truth. When she looked up, she noticed that she'd somehow gotten in front of Peter and had almost reached their dads.

By the time they reached the barn, Olive felt a little more settled. The barn and the orchard always made her feel better somehow.

The barn did not look haunted yet—it looked filled with people still alive, pounding nails, lifting props, yelling to each other, and generally causing chaos. To the side, Gloria and at least five of her friends stood in a circle, doing something weird with their voices. Gloria's words carried to them: "Let the spirit of the season take hold of you—let the noises that need to come out, come out!"

Olive saw her dad John snicker, and Olive smiled too. She glanced at Peter to share a look with him, but his face had broken into a huge grin and he started walking faster to the barn. Olive followed his gaze and saw Lizzie and Sarah having a heated discussion outside the barn doors. Olive broke off from her dads with a quick wave and followed Peter toward their friends.

As she and Peter got closer, Sheriff Hadley tiptoed up behind Sarah. He saw Olive and Peter and put his finger to his lips. His red hair was sticking straight up and his hands were covered in black paint. But per usual, he had a twinkle in his eye and a mischievous smile on his face. Olive smiled and nodded.

Right then, Sarah and Lizzie noticed Peter and Olive. Sarah said, "There you are. You guys need to take a vote: Lizzie here thinks we should stick to Nerf darts to shoot at the zombies, but I think we should use paint balls because those hit harder and will look more convincing. What do you—"

But her words were cut off by a loud ROOOAARRR behind her. Sheriff Hadley's eyes were wide and pretend-fierce, and his arms were up like a big ghoul's, looming over Sarah. She turned around fast and screamed loudly— higher and more loudly than Olive had ever heard her yell before. But as she screamed, she threw her fist out and punched Sheriff Hadley right in the chin.

"Argh!" yelled the sheriff at the same time that Sarah yelled, "GET AWAY, MONSTER!"

Finally, Sarah seemed to realize it was the sheriff, and she said, "Oh. It's just you." She shook her hand. "Your chin is hard," she said.

Meanwhile, Peter, Lizzie, and Olive dissolved in laughter.

The sheriff rubbed his chin ruefully. "I suppose this serves me right," he said, winking at the gang.

Sarah put her hands on her hips. "It sure does."

Sheriff Hadley patted Sarah on the shoulder. "I pity any monsters that come across you, Sarah," he said.

From across the barn, Sarah's mom called out, "Colin, quit terrorizing the girls and finish this loft with me." Sheriff Hadley gave them one last grin and then walked back into the barn.

The space was filled with townspeople and activity. Annabelle from Annabelle's Antiques sat with a Victorian parasol on a hay bale and called out directions. She yelled out, "Do this well, everyone, and I'll treat you to a poem!" Olive had heard her poems before. She would argue with the term "treat."

Hakeem from the hardware store and Stella from Stella's Imported Goods hammered something in the corner—what looked like a circus tent entrance—and Dinah from the diner used her cane to clear hay from a space on the floor. Aaron and Noa, from Noa's Grocery and Bait, moved a table to the newly cleared space, while Rachel, Aaron's wife and co-owner of Dinah's

Diner, painted something in the corner. Olive saw Dani, the town's mayor, with her wife and Community Spirit leader, Kate; Aldo and Mariko from the farm store; and the town's postman, Faiyaz. For a second, she smiled hugely to herself. She'd never been to a town where everyone helped out. Her dads had said the same thing— New Amity was different. She loved their new town and all the people in it.

A loud "*OUCH!*" wiped the smile off Olive's face. Hakeem shook his thumb and dropped his hammer. Stella flapped around him, trying to get him a Band-Aid. Peter moved closer to Olive and said, "Lizzie says that's the third time Hakeem's hammered his thumb."

Olive laughed a little. "He should really stop hammering."

20

Lizzie and Sarah walked up. Sarah said, "It's just weird. Hakeem owns a hardware store and builds things all the time. I heard him tell Stella he felt kind of fuzzy today. It's a little creepy."

Lizzie said, "Yeah, this barn has a . . ."

Sarah finished, "Weird feel to it."

Peter nodded, and Olive fought the urge to groan. She said, "What do you mean, 'weird feel'?"

Lizzie said, her eyes wide, "I don't know. Just, something seems . . . off."

The moment she said that, they heard a shout and saw someone roll out of the loft. Sheriff Hadley rushed to the edge and looked down. "ANA!" he yelled. He looked like he was ready to jump out of the loft right there. Sarah had already started to run to the scene. But

Olive saw a long brown arm shoot up and heard a muffled, "I'm okay!" Sarah's mom popped up and brushed hay off her clothes. Sarah reached her, and her mother put her arm around her. "Well, we know the skit will work now!" Sarah's mom said. "Whoever plays the victim and is 'pushed' off will be just fine." She looked up at Sheriff Hadley and grinned. "I would even say that was fun."

Sarah giggled. "I want to do that!" She started picking hay off her mom's clothes.

Her mom squeezed her shoulder. "Let's leave that to the professional actors over there." She pointed to Gloria and the group of her friends who had come into the barn at her yell. "At least we got the speakers and the microphones in for the play before I fell. Our actors will have the spooky music they need and the louder voices for their craft." She winked at Peter, Lizzie, and Olive.

Another yell came from a different corner of the barn. This time it was Aaron, who was jumping up and down on one foot. Rachel had gotten up and was trying to get him to stop so she could see. "I'm fine, I'm fine, I'm fine . . . ," he said, and put his foot down gingerly. He practiced walking a few steps. "I have no idea how that thing fell off the table! It was in the middle of it—how could it fall off and hit my foot?" Rachel patted his shoulder. "I'm sure it was a ghost," she said, her smile mischievous. He grinned and brought her close to kiss her, and then leaned on her as he limped to a hay bale to sit down.

Lizzie whispered, "See what I mean about

'off'? People keep getting hurt here. It's almost like this barn is . . ."

Peter and Sarah said at the same time, "Cursed."

Olive groaned this time. She couldn't help herself. The too-tight feeling was too much. "There's NO SUCH THING AS—"

Before Olive could finish, a voice said right near her ear, "Not cursed. HAUNTED."

Gloria had her sunglasses down and stared right into Olive's eyes. She looked away and said, "Follow me if you want to hear the story of Verity Wentworth, the ghost of Garrison Orchard." Then she walked out the barn doors. Lizzie, Peter, and Sarah shared an excited look, then followed her.

Olive swallowed her frustration. She could

either stay in the barn by herself or follow her brother and her friends out to listen to a ghost story.

She guessed she'd be hearing the story of Verity Wentworth, then. The ghost of Garrison Orchard.

CHAPTER 3
This Doesn't Seem Verity True

Gloria walked out of the barn and past her friends. She pulled her sunglasses down and gave them a look—a look that evidently said, "Stay here," because they all nodded and didn't move.

She kept walking until she got to the picnic table by the creek. The leaves on the trees had just started to turn colors, so the area was lit in yellows, oranges, and reds. The branches loomed over the table and cast shadows on it and on the ground all around it. Gloria sat on one side of the picnic table and the four of them crammed onto the other bench. Olive stole a glance at her brother and her two friends—they all leaned toward Gloria, their eyes wide. Olive sighed and shook her head.

"Babies," Gloria started, pulling her sunglasses down her nose to look at them. "This tale I'm about to tell you will be upsetting. Possibly so upsetting to babies of your particular age that you should not hear it. Do you pledge to me that you are fit and of sound mind enough to hear this gruesome tale?"

Olive sighed again. Lizzie nodded, and so did Peter. Sarah said, "OH HECK YEAH." Gloria looked at Olive. Then Lizzie, Peter, and Sarah all looked at her expectantly too.

"What?" Olive said loudly. "Fine, I guess. Whatever." Peter gave her a look, but she ignored it. She didn't know why she felt so frustrated—she just did.

Gloria seemed to be satisfied by this and took her sunglasses off completely. She set them down on the table and leaned in. A wind blew from somewhere, making the trees shake and skittering leaves across the ground. Olive shivered a little and wrapped her jacket tighter around herself. She wondered why it seemed just a little darker under the trees all of a sudden.

"All right then. This is the story—never told before—of Verity Wentworth and her tragic end. Long ago, when this orchard was in its much younger days, it belonged to a family called the Wentworths. Now, the Wentworths were a small family—they had one daughter and one younger son. In those days, large families were needed for farming, and the Wentworths were no exception. But their daughter, Verity, was a hard worker. She loved the land and the barn and the animals. She loved planting the trees and watching them grow year after year. She loved her brother and her mom and dad, and she would do anything, anything at all, to keep their lives happy and stable on the beautiful land they called home."

Now Olive interrupted. "I mean, it wasn't their home. It was really Native American land, but . . ."

All five of them nodded, and Gloria said, "Indeed."

They were all silent for a moment, and the wind picked up, making a moaning sound in the trees, leading Olive to shiver again.

Gloria said, "But for now, we will tell Verity's story." She cleared her throat and went on, "As she grew older and reached marriage age—what was marriage age then, anyway—many townsmen tried to court her. But Verity wasn't interested. All she was interested in was planting the trees and the crops, taking care of the animals, and helping out her family for the rest of her life. Nothing meant more to her. Nothing." Gloria took a dramatic breath. "But then tragedy struck.

"One day, Verity's father was working the land when a snake came out of nowhere. Verity's father's trusty horse reared up and took off out of the field—dragging Verity's father with him. The reins around her father's wrists held tight, and her father was dragged for almost a mile before they broke. But the reins weren't the only thing that broke. When he was finally free, her father had a broken arm, a broken leg, and a serious head wound that knocked him out cold. When they got him back to the house, he could barely move."

Olive felt herself lean forward across the picnic table too. She swallowed.

"The tragedy was not just that the poor man had been so badly hurt," Gloria said, "but that the farm and the orchard no longer had its burliest and most experienced worker. Without Mr. Wentworth, the entire season would be lost and the family would surely starve. They needed farmhands immediately. But they had one big problem—they had no way to pay them. Verity lost sleep trying to think of things the family could do to save itself.

"It was around this time that a wealthy banker

and nobleman noticed Verity. Baron von Steuben fell in love with Verity—or what passed for love with him—the first time he laid eyes on her. He wanted her to be his wife, and no other. Surely she would marry him, he thought, if only for his money. The family was in dire straits, after all. As he spoke with Verity's parents, he changed his request into a demand. 'I'm here,' he said, looking down his nose at them, 'to make Verity my wife. I assume you will have no objections. As soon as we are married, I'll fix up this scrappy little farm, I suppose. Then we'll see what's to be done.' He walked out of the house, not waiting for any response, certain of his future, happiness dancing in his wicked heart."

Sarah said, "He sounds like a jerk!"

Glory nodded solemnly. "Yes, that he was."

Lizzie whispered, "I hope she doesn't marry him. . . ." Olive found herself nodding.

Gloria continued, "Down the path from the house, Baron von Steuben ran into Verity, his soon-to-be wife. 'Good day, my dear,' he said, his eyes wide and assured. 'I've just visited with your parents. It seems I have their blessing to ask for your hand, seeing as though this is the only way this scrawny little farm could possibly survive. I'll let you plan the wedding—I understand that women dream of their weddings their whole lives."

Gloria shifted on the picnic table bench and leaned back. "Now, remember, Baron von Steuben was rich. Richer than anyone else in town. One of the richest people in the land at the time. He was not used to the word 'no.' Luckily, Verity did not use the word 'no.'

"But unluckily, she did the worst thing she could have done: she laughed at him."

Peter said, "He deserved it, that's for sure."

Gloria raised an eyebrow. "He did deserve it. But people like Baron von Steuben are surrounded by people who tell them what they want to hear all the time."

"Why?" Olive asked. "Why would he pick friends like that?"

Peter said quietly, "Sometimes people just want to feel like they're cool." Olive thought she knew what he was talking about. His brief friendship with a phony a while back had made him wiser than he should be.

Gloria nodded. "Yes, cool. And adored. And they want to believe that they are better than other people. Baron von Steuben wanted all of these things and more. He believed that he deserved to get whatever he wanted, whenever. So when Verity Wentworth laughed at him, his rage knew no bounds.

"'And what are you laughing at, little missy?' he sputtered. Verity let her laugh die down and composed herself. 'What a generous offer, sir,' she said. 'But I will not be marrying you.' She began walking down the path again. He grabbed her arm, but she yanked it away and glared at him. 'Excuse me, sir, but you are no gentleman to handle a lady in such a way!' Now Baron von Steuben laughed. 'A lady? Indeed. I could make you a lady. But if you refuse my offer, not only will you not be a lady, you will be destitute and starving. And dead before you know it. You and your family!"

Sarah whispered to Lizzie, "What does 'destitute' mean?"

Olive said, "It means poor." Lizzie nodded and Sarah said, "Okay."

Gloria went on, "Just then, a group of people appeared, walking toward the baron and Verity. The group carried all sorts of things. They carried hoes and rakes, shovels and plows. They carried baskets of food and jars of preserves. They carried, in short, the things the Wentworths needed. The baron's eyes grew wide. Verity, smiling a little, said, 'I don't believe that will happen, sir. You see, this town has heard of our situation. We won't be needing your help.' And with that, she gathered her skirts and walked away, leaving Baron von Steuben stewing."

CHAPTER 4
The Origin of the Curse

Gloria put on her sunglasses again and looked up at the trees. "The trees know . . . ," she said, trailing off.

Olive furrowed her eyebrows. "Know what?" she asked.

Gloria moved her hand lazily around. "Everything." But then she leaned in suddenly. "They know what happened that night. That fateful night."

All four of them leaned toward Gloria again.

"All day the people of the town helped the Wentworths. They harvested crops, they tended to trees, they took care of the animals. The Wentworths were fed, and the family and the townspeople celebrated that night with cider and with music, into the wee hours of the morning. Verity Wentworth knew that all would be well— the townspeople would help them until they got back on their feet. And they would do the same for anyone in town once they were back on their feet. Verity went to sleep that night, warm and happy, without a thought about the wicked Baron von Steuben.

"The next morning she woke up to a smell. Groggy, Verity turned over in her bed and looked out the window, and she saw it: smoke. She sat up straight, rushed to put on her shoes, and, still in her nightgown, she ran to the field. All the trees burned in their rows; bright flames tore through the barn and burned on the cellar door; the barn doors stood open and animals streamed out. Verity rushed to the well, yelling for her mother and brother to come help put the fire out. After hours and hours of throwing buckets on flames, the fires finally stopped burning. But what was left was a field of scorched trees, an empty cellar, and a partially burned barn.

"Verity sank down on the road in exhaustion. Far up on a hill, she saw the outline of a man on a horse, and she knew: this was the work of Baron von Steuben. She called her brother over to her tiredly. 'Jacob, please go find Baron von Steuben. Tell him to meet me at the barn at dusk to discuss his marriage proposal.' Jacob began to protest, but Verity shushed him. Her mother, Prudence, said, 'Verity, we will find another way,' but Verity shook her head. 'I just want to talk to him. I want to bring him here to see the damage he has done. I will beg him to leave us alone, and I will appeal to his humanity.' She stood up and brushed off her skirts. She smoothed down her hair and wiped the tears off her face. She looked at her mother and brother and her eyes turned hard. She said, 'But mark my words. I will die before I will marry Baron von Steuben.' Then she walked away and began to salvage what she could of the burned farm.

"Dusk came and Verity walked quickly to the barn. She had warned off her brother and mother—she knew that Baron von Steuben, coward that he was, would not show up if others were there too. She climbed to the hayloft and sat on a bale, thinking of how to word her plea. Surely the man, even as wicked as he was, would show some mercy. Surely she could find the magic words that would stop his cruelty.

"But dusk came and went and there was no sign of Baron von Steuben. Verity fell asleep on the hay waiting, and hours later, she woke up to the detestable man standing over her, a cruel smile on his face. 'I see you've come to your senses, Verity.' She stood up tall, trying to shake the sleep from her head. An anger burned in her as bright as the fires that had ravaged her family's farm. She knew she was looking at the culprit. 'Baron von Steuben, was it you who set the fires?' she asked, her voice strong and unwavering. Baron

43

von Steuben laughed a cruel laugh and stepped closer to her. Verity could not step back without falling over the hay bale, so she stood even taller. He said, 'Good deduction, my dear. And now you know—nothing stops me from getting what I want. If you agree to marriage, I will stop. If you do not, it will only get worse from here.'

"Ugh!" Sarah said. "This guy is the worst!" Peter, Lizzie, and Olive nodded.

"Poor Verity . . . ," Lizzie said.

Gloria said, "Now Verity took a step forward, so surprising Baron von Steuben that he stumbled back. 'Get this through your thick head—I will never, ever, ever marry you. I asked you to come here to appeal to your humanity. To ask you to stop these wicked attacks. But now I see you are not human—you are a monster. I would rather be dead than spend one minute of my life with you.' Baron von Steuben's face turned bright red. The barn seemed to darken, and the lamp Verity had brought with her dimmed, as if a wicked wind sought to blow it out. Baron von Steuben took a deep breath and, in one swift move, grabbed Verity Wentworth and threw her out of the hayloft. 'Then dead you shall be,' he hissed."

Olive gasped and realized she wasn't the only one. Everyone was on the edge of their seats.

Gloria's voice got low. "A terrible quiet took over the barn. No crickets sang outside, no owls hooted. And Baron von Steuben realized what he'd done. He looked out of the loft and saw Verity Wentworth on the floor of the barn, where no hay had broken her fall. Her neck was bent at an unnatural angle, and one eye was open. He had killed her."

Peter, Lizzie, Sarah, and even Olive exhaled at the same time. "Poor Verity!" Lizzie said again.

Peter looked mad, even through his normally thoughtful expression. "That's an evil act," he said, shaking his head.

Gloria nodded and said, "Oh, yes. But even more evil were Baron von Steuben's next actions. Thinking quickly, he ran to the house and knocked on the door. Prudence Wentworth, Verity's mother, answered, still sleepy. When she saw him, her eyes widened and she tried to shut the door, but Baron von Steuben caught it with his foot. 'No, Mrs. Wentworth, I mean you no harm. I came to meet Verity at the barn, but wanted to prove my innocence before I came. Alas, I could not find the culprits who started the fire, but I did find'—and here he broke down into an admirable crying fit, a fit that only the best of actors could have pulled off, and said, 'I did find Verity, dead. Thrown from the hayloft. I suspect the real culprit came and killed her.' He choked on a fake sob and checked with one eye to see if Prudence had bought his act.

"But Prudence only cared about her daughter. She ran to the barn, her son running after her, and together they found Verity on the ground. They collapsed, heartbroken. And Baron von Steuben went to the town to tell everyone the news—his version—blaming some unknown assailant for his evil deed. Though the Wentworths never believed him, the story of Verity's murder by a stranger grew—spurred on by the evil Baron von Steuben—until it became a local legend. And over the years, the story took many new forms. Verity killed herself. Verity was killed by a demon. Verity saw a ghost and fell . . . but the real story of Verity Wentworth's murder was buried with her, so that the awful, cruel, wicked Baron von Steuben got away with it."

Here Gloria's voice got even lower, and she looked around, as if making sure no one else was listening. "To this day, Verity Wentworth haunts the barn, trying to find a way to tell her story. And until she can, accidents befall all those who dare work on her beloved farm, in her beloved barn."

Gloria put her sunglasses back on. Lizzie, Peter, and Sarah all exhaled at the same time. They all looked around as if expecting Verity

Wentworth to show up right beside them.

But Olive was stuck on something. It was one of the last things that Gloria had told them. "Wait," she said, her eyebrows furrowing.

Gloria pulled her sunglasses down and looked at Olive. "Yes?" she said, her tone condescending and irritated.

Olive said, "If no one knows her story, how did you just tell it to us?"

CHAPTER 5
Making Hay

What are you talking about?" Gloria asked, pushing her sunglasses back up.

"How can you know what the story is if it's never been told?" Olive said again. She felt triumphant. She had to admit, she'd been into that story. She had even gotten goose bumps. But now she was back on firm ground.

Ghosts weren't real.

She sat up straighter. "And furthermore,

if she's been haunting this barn for years, why hasn't anyone ever heard of it?" She turned to Lizzie. "Have YOU ever seen anything or heard anything that shows the barn is haunted by Verity Wentworth?"

"Well . . ." Lizzie trailed off. For some reason that Olive couldn't fathom, she looked disappointed. "I guess not?"

Sarah jumped in. "We normally don't play in the barn. I bet we felt somehow that it was haunted!"

"Yeah," Lizzie said, her voice growing stronger. "It was always too dangerous to go in. So we didn't until recently."

Now Peter chimed in. "And accidents have been happening ever since, right?"

Olive couldn't believe her ears. "Peter," she

said, but then didn't know quite what to say. She looked around at her friends and saw the hopeful looks on their faces. That too-tight feeling came again. Something was not sitting right.

So she said what was really on her mind: "Why would you believe this stuff? I thought you were smarter than this."

Everyone got quiet, and Olive swallowed. She saw that Lizzie had tears in her eyes. Sarah glared at her. Peter looked disappointed.

"I'm sorry, I just . . . I don't understand why you're pretending this stuff is real . . . ," Olive said as her eyes filled. She knew she'd gone too far. She couldn't stand the looks her friends and her brother were giving her. And at the same time, she felt indignant. She was right. Was she the only sane one sitting there?

Gloria stood up and stepped away from the picnic table. "Believe what you will. I, however, am an actress. We sensitive souls, unlike YOU"— she glared at Olive—"can feel things that most people cannot. I have gathered Verity's story from the ether—I simply KNOW things." Then she turned on her heel and yelled, "ACTING!" and walked away.

Sarah got up and stepped over the picnic table bench. "Sometimes, Olive, you can be really mean." She shook her head and began walking toward the barn.

Lizzie got up too and shot Olive a hurt look. "I'm not dumb," she said. She followed Sarah.

Olive pushed her glasses up and then got up too. "Lizzie . . . Sarah," she called, but she didn't really have anything to say.

Peter got up. "Olive. You're my sister. But you're not making it easy to hang out with you." He turned away.

Olive said, a tear trailing down her cheek, "So I'm just supposed to pretend I think something is true? Even if it's ridiculous?"

Peter sighed. "There are other things that are important, you know," he told her. He walked away, leaving Olive alone at the picnic table.

She took off her glasses and wiped away the tears. With one big sniffle, she put on her glasses again. She would go to the barn and ask her dads if she could go home. She clearly was alone in all of this. The thought made tears squeeze from her eyes again.

She looked up ahead as she walked, seeing three of her favorite people in the world talking and having fun without her. They had almost made it to the barn, and as Olive got closer, she could hear the hammering and the talking and the laughter inside. The sun had begun to set, and rays of light streamed through the boards at the other end of the barn. Just as Olive almost reached her three friends, she heard a sharp yell.

Looking up, she saw the outline of Sheriff Hadley in the hayloft, just where Ms. Shirvani had been. He teetered on the edge, waving his arms and trying to catch his balance. Olive ran up beside Peter and her friends, and just as she did, Sheriff Hadley plummeted to the ground.

A collective gasp went through the crowd in the barn as people rushed to his aid.

Ms. Shirvani's voice carried over toward them: "Where is the hay that was here? When I fell, I fell into some hay! What happened?"

Sheriff Hadley groaned, and Hakeem yelled, "We need to call an ambulance!"

Olive caught eyes with Lizzie, Sarah, and Peter. A few moments later, as people bustled around her and they heard a siren approaching, Olive heard someone say, "It looks like he was pushed." Another person Olive couldn't see said, "Yeah, I saw that too. It was like something knocked him over."

And then a voice replied, "But he was up there alone."

The sound of the siren filled the barn as the ambulance pulled up to carry Sheriff Hadley to the hospital.

CHAPTER 6
A Plan

It totally looked like he was pushed off somehow," Peter said, grabbing another piece of French toast. "A lot of people said that." He looked at Olive like he expected her to challenge him.

She didn't say anything. She hadn't really said anything to him all morning. Part of it was because she felt bad about saying what she had at the picnic table yesterday; but also, she'd started to get mad. Mad that she was the one who made sense and they were the ones who didn't, but still somehow, she was made to feel like the jerk. It didn't seem fair. She put a piece of the French toast on her plate and poured syrup on it. A little dribbled on her hand and she licked it off.

Her dad David said, "Hmm. That sounds scary. Is the sheriff all right?"

Peter said, "Sarah's going to call us with an update. But he was talking when the ambulance took him away, so I don't think it's super-serious."

As if Peter had summoned the call, their cell phone (Peter and Olive shared one) rang in the living room. Everyone in the dining room looked at John. It was against the rules, big-time, to answer the phone during any meal. And breakfast on a Sunday morning was pretty sacred in their household. But John nodded, and Peter sprinted to get the call.

He looked at the phone and answered, "Hey, Sarah. What's up?" He said, "Uh-huh. Yeah. Okay. Good. Yeah. In a bit." Then he glanced at Olive. "Yeah, she'll probably want to. Even though we're dumb . . . See you in a bit!" He put the phone in his pocket and came back to the table. He sat down and took a big bite of his French toast.

Olive fumed. She knew what Sarah had said. But she hadn't even said they were dumb! Just that she thought they were smarter than believing in things that didn't exist . . . She stared at Peter and then said finally, "Well?"

Peter said around the bite of French toast, "Sheriff Hadley broke his arm, but he's okay. Sarah asked him if it felt like he was pushed and he said he didn't really remember. But because of all the accidents that've been happening, everyone's taking a break from the barn." He finished chewing and swallowed.

Their dad John gave him a look—not speaking with a full mouth was another mealtime rule. Peter smiled sheepishly and said, "Sorry. This breakfast is good. Anyway, Sarah and Lizzie want to meet up and go talk to townspeople today. Can Olive and I go? I mean, if Olive wants to." He took another big bite.

Of course she wanted to go. They were her friends.

She'd thought.

She took a big bite of her own French toast to hide her hurt. Just because she had a different opinion didn't mean she should be excluded from things. Maybe she shouldn't have said what she did . . . but that didn't mean she wasn't still their friend.

"I might not go," she said, trying to sound nonchalant. She felt a sharp look from Peter as if it were physical, but she didn't look at him. She kept chewing.

David said, "Is something wrong?"

She shrugged. "No."

Everyone at the table was silent for a minute, and then Peter spoke. "Whatever. I'm going to go."

Olive chewed for a while and then took a drink of her juice. Staying at home would be . . . hard. Harder than going. "I guess I'll go too," she said.

"Whatever," Peter said. He got up and put his plate in the sink, not meeting eyes with Olive. She could feel her dads' eyes on her and

Peter—it wasn't like them to fight.

To stave off any questions, she put her plate in the sink too and said, "Fine. Let's go."

Peter and Olive walked fast to Annabelle's Antiques, where they were meeting Lizzie and Sarah. They walked fast because Peter was walking fast, and Olive had to hurry to keep up. He was definitely mad. But that was fine: SHE was mad too. When they reached the store, Lizzie and Sarah came walking around the corner of the building, waving.

Olive realized that she hadn't asked what they were doing. She also realized that everyone seemed nervous. She knew she did. She was having a hard time looking them in the eyes.

She cleared her throat and said, "What are we doing?"

Sarah, not looking at her, said, "We're investigating to see if the Verity story is true. Since SOME of us are so smart and skeptical."

Olive rolled her eyes. Anger burned in her. She mumbled, "It IS smart to be skeptical. . . ."

Lizzie squeaked, "We could find something that tells us about Verity. Or not! Either way, it will be fun because we're together." But her face looked strained, and now Olive did feel bad. Lizzie didn't look like she was having fun at all. Olive knew Lizzie hated it when people fought. She thought about how much she liked Lizzie and didn't want her to feel bad.

She took a deep breath. "Okay. That sounds like fun. We might find out something about the story. . . ."

Sarah shifted. "Well, we thought you made a

good point yesterday. About Gloria knowing the story when it was supposedly never told before . . ."

Olive cleared her throat and pushed up her glasses. She nodded and tried not to look like she'd told them so.

Sarah rolled her eyes a little, so Olive figured she hadn't quite kept the "I told you so" look off her face. But Sarah went on, "So we thought we'd ask some of the townspeople if they've heard of this story. We thought that might be the *smart* thing to do."

Olive said, her voice low, "I shouldn't have said that. I think you're all smart." She went on quickly so no one could say anything. "Did Gloria say how she heard the story? Won't she just tell you?"

Lizzie shrugged. "No way. I can barely get her to look at me when I'm in the same room with her." She smiled sheepishly. Olive didn't know what that was like, having an older sibling. It sounded like it was complicated. Then again, having a twin felt complicated today too. Same with having friends.

"Okay, let's start with Annabelle!" Sarah said. Olive breathed a sigh of relief. Maybe their fight was behind them.

Sarah turned around and walked into the store. Lizzie and Peter followed. Olive could feel herself tensing. She didn't know exactly why, but she hoped Annabelle didn't know anything about the story. She shook off the feeling of being a bad friend and followed her crew into the store. She'd already said one fairly bad thing to them. She had to remember what Peter had said: sometimes there were other things to worry about than just being right.

CHAPTER 7
Deeds Aren't Proof

Annabelle bustled between the shelves, picking up dusty book after dusty book. Her Victorian skirts brushed the floor and she muttered to herself. Olive stayed far back—it seemed like Annabelle was possessed. When they'd asked her if she'd ever heard of Verity Wentworth, her eyes had gotten wide. "No," she'd said. "But if she exists, I shall find her."

Twenty minutes later, Peter, Olive, Lizzie,

and Sarah stared as Annabelle took down almost every antique book and thumbed through each one carefully. "In a year or two, I'll be donating these books to a library, where they can keep them temperature-controlled. But I just haven't been able to make myself do it yet."

Finally, Annabelle took a seat on an antique settee. She fanned herself. "It appears my books don't reach into the past quite that far. I could have sworn I had a town charter. . . . But then again, New Amity was made up of many different small towns and farms back then, so a town charter was nary a glimmer in anyone's eye." She took out a handkerchief and dabbed at her temples. "My, that search was quite the calisthenics session."

Olive had to stifle a giggle. But she had to admit, Annabelle did look really hot in all those layers.

Sarah said, "Do you have any other ideas about where we can look?"

Annabelle smiled. "Why, I'd ask your dear mother, Sarah. She is the town librarian, after all. And a fine historian as well."

Olive looked at Sarah. "She's a historian, too?"

Sarah shrugged. "I don't know. I only know I have to help her shelve things. Okay, we'll check with her later. Come on, guys." She waved her hand at them and they all followed her.

"Where to next?" Peter asked.

No one spoke for a second. Sarah took a breath like she was going to say something, but Lizzie jumped in. "I say we try for the mayor. Let's talk to Dani."

Sarah looked surprised but then said, "Yeah. That's a good idea."

Olive liked that idea too. "Let's do that," she said. She hoped Mayor Alvarez would back her up. The four of them walked along Main Street, seeing Hakeem and Stella chatting outside the hardware store. They saw Rachel and Aaron with a stroller walking across the street. Everyone waved at them as they passed. Noa from the grocery store, Faiyaz, Mariko and Aldo . . . they all said hi or waved. Olive still couldn't believe how nice everyone in this town was. At the end of Main Street sat the town hall. Every Sunday morning there was a Community Spirit service there. Sometimes Olive and Peter and their dads went, but sometimes they just ate French toast. Today had been a French toast day.

"Would Dani still be here?" Olive asked. It was already one thirty, past the time of the service.

"Oh, yeah. She and Kate stay to clean up," Lizzie said.

When they reached the building, they heard singing, and they opened the doors. Kate and Dani were dancing and laughing together, Dani belting out a tune. Lizzie blushed and giggled. Peter laughed too, and Sarah practically fell over laughing. Olive stifled her chuckle.

Dani stopped singing when the door opened, but instead of looking embarrassed, she looked delighted. "Sarah! Lizzie! Peter and Olive!" she said, kissing Kate on the cheek and then dropping her hands. "Come on in! What can we help you with?"

Olive couldn't help but return the mayor's infectious smile. She decided she wanted to do the talking here. Even though Sarah had said she'd had a good point, Olive wasn't sure Sarah would be totally objective if she asked the questions. Olive said, "We're looking for information on someone who probably didn't live here long ago. Verity Wentworth—do you know anyone by that name who was here in the earlier days of this town?"

She could feel Peter's eyes on her, but she ignored him.

Dani pursed her lips and narrowed her eyes. "That name doesn't sound familiar. . . . But I keep some old documents in my office upstairs. Any reason why you're looking for this woman? A woman who probably didn't live here?" Her mouth twitched in a tiny smile.

Olive said, "They think she's a ghost," at the same time that Peter said, "No reason."

One look at Lizzie, Sarah, and Peter told Olive she'd just made another error. This time she didn't really understand—it was the truth! But still, she was already in trouble with them. She swallowed. "No reason," she said.

Dani waved them over. "Come on up!" She started up the stairs, and the group followed her. Kate called up, "There are cookies downstairs when you're through!"

The four of them crowded into Dani's office as she took out a black box. She unlocked it, and Olive saw a whole bunch of papers sitting in it. "Here are some photocopies I took a long time ago with some of our town votes. Let me see if we have anything that has her name. Around what time period?"

Lizzie looked at Sarah. They both shrugged.

Peter said, "Around the late eighteenth or early nineteenth century."

Olive knew he loved these sorts of things. When they'd first moved to New Amity, Peter had pretty much memorized everything about the history of the town. And his memory was always spot-on. She felt a familiar wave of pride go through her.

"Okay . . . ," Dani murmured. She sifted through the papers and then stopped at one. She leaned down and squinted. Then she handed the paper to Sarah. "Can you read that?"

Sarah squinted at it too. "It looks like . . . 'w-e-n-t-w-a' . . . but then it's cut off."

Lizzie leaned in. "That could be an 'o.' So it is 'w-e-n-t-w-o' . . ."

Peter nodded. "That could definitely be

'Wentworth.' What is this, Mayor Alvarez?"

Dani said, "It's a vote about becoming a town and naming it New Amity. This is in the early eighteen hundreds. Right around the time the town became a town. And please call me Dani." She smiled at them all.

Olive leaned in and looked at the paper. The name they were talking about was written in ornate script. It was hard to read, and it had indeed gotten cut off. In fact, most of the names were hard to read.

"Wait! What's that?" Peter pointed to a paper sitting on Dani's desk. He leaned in and said, "This is some sort of deed for a Baron von Steuben." He stood straight up and said, "BARON VON STEUBEN."

Dani looked confused. Lizzie, Sarah, and

Peter all said, "Whoooooaaaa," at the same time. And Olive had to admit she got goose bumps.

But that didn't prove anything.

"That doesn't prove anything," she said, trying to make her voice sound not-defensive.

Sarah looked at her and smiled. "But you have to admit, it gets us closer!"

Dani looked from Sarah to Olive to Peter to Lizzie, all with a smile on her face. She said, "Who is Baron von Steuben?"

Olive huffed out. "He's part of this story that they all want to believe about a ghost. But I know it's not true. Because ghosts don't exist. That deed doesn't prove anything." She looked at Dani.

And then Dani said, "Well, we don't know everything, do we? Who knows? Maybe keeping an open mind about this might be fun?" She winked at Olive.

Olive didn't have to look at Peter to know he was smiling. And she wouldn't look at the rest of them.

Now even grown-ups were being dumb. Olive sat down and crossed her arms over her chest.

CHAPTER 8

Accidents Waiting to Happen

All the way back to the Garrison Orchard, Olive was quiet. She felt like crying again and she just didn't understand why. She could feel Peter's eyes on her, but she kept looking at the ground, letting everyone else talk.

Finally, right at the end of the Garrisons' driveway, Sarah stopped short. "Okay, Olive, what is going on? Are you mad at us?"

Olive looked up in surprise and pushed her

glasses up on her nose. She thought for a minute. She was mad at them. REALLY mad. But she had no idea why.

She took a deep breath and tried to put it into words. "It's just . . . why . . . how . . . I don't get why you guys want to believe in this baby stuff," she finally said.

Peter said, "Olive, why do you have to be so mean about this?" His voice was frustrated, which hardly ever happened.

Olive looked out. "I don't know!" she said, her voice getting louder. "Why do you like this stuff?"

"I thought you liked it too," Lizzie said quietly.

That stopped Olive. She had liked it. She had loved the idea of a zombie hayride and a haunted barn. She still did. She just felt like the only one who wasn't crazy. "I just . . . I never thought this stuff was real, I guess."

Sarah huffed out. "We don't know if it is! What does it hurt to try to find out?"

Olive had no answer for that. What did it hurt? Just as she was about to respond, Peter said, "Uh, Lizzie, why are your horses just standing in the driveway?" At the same time, Sarah said, "Is that smoke I smell?"

They all looked up. Two of the Garrisons' horses stood in the driveway—which was super-weird. Olive saw smoke in the back field where the pumpkins were. Albert and Tabitha stood in the yard yelling directions to some farmhands, while others rushed to the back field. Sirens wailed, and the four kids jumped out of the way as a fire truck turned into the driveway. Olive glanced at the barn, which stood with sunlight streaming around it. There appeared to be nothing wrong with it at all. But everything else at the Garrisons' seemed to be caught up in some sort of chaos. As the four of them walked to the house, Olive looked at the wraparound front porch. Tabitha and Albert had now stopped yelling directions and were talking to one of the firefighters at the bottom of the steps. Other firefighters unspooled a long hose.

As Olive watched, a light on the porch turned on, then burned brightly.

Then exploded.

Everyone screamed and ducked.

Lizzie's eyes had grown round and alarmed. Olive felt a shiver of fear as she straightened up.

"What the heck . . . ?" she started.

Sarah finished, ". . . is going on?"

Out of nowhere, a voice said near Olive, "It's Verity. She's not satisfied with just the barn anymore."

Olive jumped so high she almost lost her shoes.

Gloria walked by them, away from the house, and smiled. It wasn't a particularly nice smile, but Olive didn't think too hard about that, because Lizzie ran to her parents and the rest of the group followed.

They reached Albert and Tabitha, and Lizzie asked, "What is happening?"

Tabitha enveloped Lizzie in a hug. "It's okay, doodlebug. We've just had a string of accidents. Something happened with the doors to the barn, so the horses got out. And then a fire started in the pumpkin patch. And now this lightbulb just exploded. But we have everything covered."

Albert said, "And the barn is fine!" He beamed at them, and Olive smiled back at him. She pushed up her glasses. "How did the fire start?" she asked.

Tabitha let go of Lizzie, and Olive saw tears in Lizzie's eyes. She felt awful for Lizzie. This orchard was everything to their family.

"We don't know how the fire started," Tabitha said. "Albert and I were in the house trying to get some decorations up and we heard a yell and saw the smoke. Then we saw one of our horses run past the house. And then Patrick, Brett, and Sally ran by. And then Karin and Jordan ran by the other window. And since that was all of our seasonal help running by our windows, we figured we should really find out what's happening.

So we came out here. Sally gave us the update."

"And then the lightbulb exploded," Albert finished.

"What can we do to help?" Peter asked. Olive was wondering the exact same thing.

"Well, I think we have everything under control now. But I would stay out of the house for a little bit. There's clearly something wrong with the electrical system," Tabitha said. "I've called the company and they're going to come out today. Thank goodness. We can't afford any more accidents!"

Olive could see that she was really worried. She wondered if she meant that literally—they couldn't afford any more accidents. She knew that putting on this seasonal show cost a lot of money up front.

Tabitha and Albert turned to talk to one of

the firefighters. Sarah's mouth set in a grim line and she said, "Come on. Let's go to the picnic table and talk about this. We've got to come up with a way to stop this haunting." Her voice went low on the word "haunting." Peter and Lizzie nodded, but Olive hesitated.

"I'm going to go for a walk," Olive said. She had to wrap her head around the accidents. She knew, just knew, that they weren't caused by a ghost. And if she could find out what they *were* caused by, maybe she could help the Garrisons.

And maybe even get her friends back.

Peter gave her a strange look. "You're going for a walk? Now?"

Olive nodded but didn't meet his eye. She did, however, catch the hurt look in Lizzie's eyes. She felt bad, but she was hoping this would help

Lizzie in the long run. So she turned and walked toward the barn.

Two of the farmhands—Patrick and Karin, Olive thought—were tending to the barn doors as the horses stood in the pasture. The horses looked nervous; when Olive approached, they whinnied and shied away. This made Olive nervous too, but a voice rang out.

"Hey there! You're Lizzie's friend, right?" Karin called.

Olive nodded. She got closer to where they were working and said, "I'm Olive."

Karin took off her work glove and extended her hand. "I'm Karin," she said as she shook Olive's hand firmly. She pointed to the stocky, friendly-looking man digging in a toolbox. "That's Patrick."

Olive waved and Patrick said, "Hiya," then went back to digging. Karin put on her work glove again and moved to one of the barn doors.

"Um . . . so, what do you think happened?" Olive asked after a minute.

Karin said, "Well, it looks like these doors were opened. But we can't figure out how. It's almost like someone did it on purpose."

Patrick brought a huge metal contraption over, and Olive could see it was a lock. The Garrisons hadn't regularly locked the barn before. This seemed serious.

"Why would somebody do that, though?" Olive asked.

Patrick shrugged. "No one would have a reason to."

Karin smiled. "Maybe a ghost did it! It's the

Halloween season, after all." She laughed at her own joke, but Olive couldn't even crack a smile.

Patrick set the lock down. "Well, I have a theory, actually," he said. Karin rolled her eyes. "She doesn't believe it, but here's what I think happened."

Karin said, "Oh, boy, here we go."

"See these two windows that are opposite each other? I think there's some strange wind pressure that happens when the weather is just right that pulls the doors in and rattles them." Patrick stopped to point at the windows and to demonstrate the rattling with his hands. "So, the wind rattles the doors and it jars the wooden bar loose so that it falls out of the latch and lets the doors open. I've said this before, but no one will believe me."

Olive knew how he felt. She got excited—that would mean it definitely wasn't a ghost. There was a perfectly logical explanation for this!

But Karin scoffed. "Right. The same day the pumpkin patch caught fire and a lightbulb exploded, the wind managed to knock the latch off the barn doors and the horses got out. Doesn't that seem like too much of a coincidence to you?"

Patrick shrugged. "It makes more sense to me than someone letting the horses out. And way more sense to me than a ghost." He winked at Olive. "Right, Olive?"

Olive nodded and grinned. Karin made a pretend-shocked face. "What? You believe him over me? I suppose you also believe the accidents in the barn are a coincidence?" She winked at Olive too, so Olive smiled back.

"I do," she said. "But my friends don't. So I'm trying to find explanations for things so I can show them that they're . . ." She was about to say so she could show them they were wrong, but that seemed, well, wrong somehow. "So I can show them there's nothing to be afraid of."

Karin laughed a little and said, "Uh-huh. That'll be helpful for them."

Olive said, "Exactly. Okay, it was nice meeting you!" She pushed her glasses up on her nose and turned to leave.

"You know . . . sometimes things can't be explained with a 'normal' explanation. We don't know everything in the world!" Karin said.

Olive closed her eyes and tried to take a deep breath.

CHAPTER 9
When Push Comes to Shove . . .

Olive decided against talking to anyone at the pumpkin patch. Or figuring out what had happened with the lightbulb. It seemed that people just wanted to believe whatever they wanted to believe—Karin was the perfect example of that. And even though Olive knew her friends were probably still irritated with her—as she was with them—she wasn't sure where else to go. She decided to meet them at the picnic table.

When she got there, Peter said, "Thanks for joining us." But he was being sarcastic. She rolled her eyes and tried to hide her hurt.

"How is everything here?" she asked.

Lizzie lit up. "We've got news!" she said. This made Olive's heart happy, and her mood lifted a little. Any good news at the moment would be amazing. Lizzie's family was going through enough.

Sarah bounced up and down on the picnic table bench and said, "Yeah! So, I called my mom about Verity Wentworth. And she said she didn't have any information because she was just an amateur historian or whatever. So she called a historian friend of hers and asked her some questions." Sarah paused and her eyes got wide. "It turns out there *was* a family called the Wentworths and there was a pamphlet that circulated about the tragic death of Verity Wentworth. The pamphlet said, get this . . ." She was looking up like she was trying to remember the exact words when Peter cut in.

"It said, 'Baron von Steuben requests any information about the wrongful death of the virtuous Verity Wentworth and offers a handsome reward of two hundred dollars.'"

Sarah nodded so hard her head looked like it might fall off. "And two hundred dollars is like a gazillion dollars back then!"

Lizzie squeaked. "The Verity story is true!"

Olive didn't say what she wanted to say. Which was that it couldn't be true. Because ghosts weren't real. But every time she opened her mouth lately, her friends got mad at her. She was tired of it. And she was tired of being the only one who felt this way. She just smiled weakly.

Peter said, "Hey, we were thinking about going to see Sheriff Hadley at the hospital. Do you want to come?"

Olive stared. Why was he constantly asking her if she wanted to come and do things with him and their two best friends? It had always been a given. "Uh, yeah," she said. "Of course."

Lizzie smiled at Olive. "I'm glad you're coming," she said. This made Olive feel worse, and she got up from the table. Like her coming was a huge favor or a weird event.

"How are we going to get there?" she asked.

Peter said, "Sarah's mom is going to come

pick us up. She wanted to visit him too."

Olive nodded again. "That makes sense."

Sarah furrowed her eyebrows. "What does that mean?"

Olive was about to answer, but she saw Lizzie's eyes widen and saw Peter shake his head a little. Olive shook her own head, exasperated. Yet another thing she couldn't be honest about. It was obvious to everyone except Sarah that her mom and Sheriff Hadley were a couple. Olive sincerely didn't understand why people had to pretend the world was one way when it clearly was another way entirely.

She shrugged. "Just that she also fell out of the loft, so they probably want to compare stories," she said.

Sarah nodded. "Oh, yeah. That's true. Hey,

we can ask him if something weird happened!"

Olive felt so tired all of a sudden. And about as old as the ghost of Verity Wentworth.

Sheriff Hadley sat up in his hospital bed, his arm in a cast and a sling and his bright red hair sticking straight up. He also looked incredibly happy—but he kind of always did. Especially when he saw Ms. Shirvani.

"Ana!" he said as they walked in the door. "And of course the awesome Sarah, the fantastic Lizzie, the amazing Peter, and the wonderful Olive!"

Even though Olive felt pretty rotten, she couldn't help smiling back at Sheriff Hadley. He was always so cheerful. And goofy-looking.

"Thanks so much for coming to visit me. I'm so bored. But the doctor says I got a concussion when I fell, so they're keeping me for observation." He picked up a Jell-O cup. "But you want to know the worst? They like to taunt me. Like they give me this Jell-O but then they won't open it for me!"

Olive giggled, and so did the rest of the group. Sheriff Hadley looked beseechingly at Ms. Shirvani. "Ana, would you mind opening this?"

Ms. Shirvani crossed her arms in front of her chest. "I don't know, Colin . . . it seems like you're going to need to learn some independence here."

He narrowed his eyes and pretended to look mad, but then Ms. Shirvani laughed and so did he. She opened his Jell-O and patted his head like he was a little kid. "Don't get used to this, though," she said, and sat down on a chair near his bed.

Olive wasn't quite sure what to do with herself. Hospitals were weird—they smelled funny and there were beeping noises going on constantly. And she felt in the way no matter where she stood. She leaned against the wall and hoped she looked natural.

Sarah said, "We want to know how you fell." Olive had to hand it to Sarah—when she wanted something, she didn't beat around the bush. Olive admired that in her. It was something they had in common.

"Ahhh. How is it that Ana here fell out of the

loft and ended up in a pile of hay, but I fell out and didn't? Well . . . the falling out was weird, I'll tell you that," the sheriff said.

Lizzie looked at all of them with big eyes, and Sarah's legs started bouncing. Peter leaned into Olive and said, "See? WEIRD."

Olive cleared her throat. This perked her up. Maybe now she could find a reasonable explanation for something. "Can you go through the whole thing?"

The sheriff looked at her with admiration. "You would be a great sheriff, you know that, Olive?"

She shuffled her feet and looked down, blushing. She had to admit, she loved the idea of being a detective. She even had a detective game that she used to play with her whole family. No one liked playing with her, though, because she always won.

"Well, Ana, do you want to tell your part?" the sheriff asked.

Ms. Shirvani nodded. "So, we were pretending to act out what the kids will act out at the end of the haunted barn. Except, we weren't going to REALLY act it out. But then I lost my balance somehow and fell. Luckily, we'd put a whole bunch of hay on the spot where the fall was supposed to be, so my landing was soft."

Lizzie asked, "How did you lose your balance, though?"

Ms. Shirvani shrugged. "I honestly don't know. I looked up to say something to Colin and then the next thing I knew, I was flying through the air."

Peter said, "And then not too long after, you fell off too, Sheriff Hadley, right?"

The sheriff nodded and swallowed the Jell-O he'd just taken a huge bite of. "Yeah, only this time, there was no hay."

Sarah said, "Someone or some THING moved it, huh?"

The sheriff laughed. "Well, I'm voting for some*one*. I think there were people in and out of there and part of their job was to make sure everything was clean. They probably moved the hay to mop the floor or something. It was just bad timing."

Olive nodded. "Yeah, a total coincidence, right?" she asked.

The sheriff nodded. "Totally." He took another bite of his Jell-O and then looked up thoughtfully. "Though . . . the fall part was weird. And a couple of other things were, too. . . ."

Peter, Lizzie, and Sarah all said, "What things?" at the same time.

Both Ms. Shirvani and the sheriff looked surprised. Olive didn't doubt it—three really intense kids asking the same question at the same time *would* be surprising.

"Well. I don't know. First of all, why was the hay only cleared off from the spot where someone would land if they fell out of the loft? That was weird. But also . . . and this may be the concussion talking . . . but it almost felt as if I were . . ."

Peter, Lizzie, and Sarah all said, ". . . pushed?"

Olive rolled her eyes. Now Ms. Shirvani and the sheriff laughed. "Geez, you kids sure are in sync today," Ms. Shirvani said. Olive didn't bother to correct her to say that only three of the kids in the room were in sync.

She spoke up. "Pushed how? Was there someone around you?"

Sheriff Hadley shook his head. "That's the thing. No one was around."

Ms. Shirvani patted his hand. "But Colin . . . you have to admit, even on a good day you're kind of clumsy."

The sheriff pretended to look offended. "That is neither here nor there, madam!" he said in mock outrage.

Ms. Shirvani giggled. "Remember that time

you fell out of your car because you tripped over your own feet? Or that time you spilled an entire bucket of paint on your own head? Or what about the time at the Comic Con festival when you lost your balance and knocked into someone, who knocked into someone else, and so on until there were five people who fell because you tripped?"

He put the spoon near his mouth, but the Jell-O slid right off onto his chest. Everyone started laughing, including him. "Well, fine. It's true. Sometimes I can be a LITTLE clumsy. So it might have just been that."

Olive looked at her friends, hoping they were starting to come around to her way of thinking, but none of them looked back at her.

"But it still felt like someone pushed you,"

Sarah said after the laughter died down.

The sheriff got serious. "It really did. Or at least, that's how I remember it. Anyway, let's forget about all that—who wants to get me some more Jell-O?"

CHAPTER 10
Aunt Willow

Outside the hospital, they were all a little uneasy. Olive felt like she was just meeting all of them for the first time. Like she'd never really known them at all, even her twin. Or at least, like she was totally different from them all of a sudden.

After an uncomfortable silence, Lizzie said, "Do you all want to come over Friday and spend the night? We can finish planning the zombie hayride and the haunted barn."

Olive relaxed a little. She still loved the idea of doing that. They had all bonded over the idea of a zombie hayride when they'd first met. She nodded. "I think our dads will let us," she said, looking at Peter. He nodded.

Sarah said, "Okay, sounds good." But her words were clipped and she didn't look at Olive. They all agreed to meet Friday night, and Olive vowed to herself that she would try to keep her mouth shut about all the ghost stuff. Even though she was right.

Peter and Olive headed off toward home to wait for the following weekend and the sleepover.

● ● ●

The two of them did their best to avoid each other for one long week, until, finally, Friday came and Olive packed her stuff for the sleepover, patted her backpack to make sure the papers she was bringing were there, and trotted down the stairs to meet her brother and their dads. She had a secret weapon in her backpack and she was feeling pretty good. She would get her friends back. And she would do it using facts and smart thinking—her normal MO.

"You ready to go?" she asked her brother cheerily.

He gave her a curious look. "Yes . . . ?"

"Good! Let's go," she said, and pushed her glasses up her nose and smiled.

John walked in, jingling his car keys. "All right, children of mine, let's get you slumbered!"

They got into the car and drove to the Garrisons'.

Sarah was already there. She and Lizzie stood on the porch, bouncing on their heels. When Peter and Olive got out of the car, Sarah squealed, "Finally! You're here!" She ran down the stairs and grabbed them both by the hands, pulling them up the stairs.

When they were all inside and had all patted the banister three times, Lizzie said, "There's a surprise here." Olive wasn't sure why they patted the banister—just that it was a tradition they observed every time they came into the house.

"Ms. G got us *Monster House* to watch!" Sarah said excitedly. "But that's not all."

Lizzie nodded, just as excited. "There's someone you should totally meet. She's the absolute best!"

Suddenly a voice Olive hadn't heard before called out from the dining room. "Well, bring them in here! I have to meet your new friends."

"It's Aunt Willow!" Sarah and Lizzie squeaked at the same time.

Peter and Olive exchanged looks. "Okay . . . ," Olive said. They had aunts too, and although they loved their aunts, they were never this excited when they visited.

"Is she famous or something?" Olive asked.

Lizzie giggled. "No. She's just really fun. Let's go to the dining room so you can meet her."

The four of them walked into the dining room, and Olive saw the most eccentrically dressed person she'd ever seen in her life.

Aunt Willow wore jeans. But she also wore at least two skirts on top of them. She had on a tank top that looked like it was made out of big leaves and had jewelry all up and down her arms. She also had tattoos here and there peeking out from behind her clothes. Her hair was long and dark, and she had huge blue eyes that looked a lot like Lizzie's. She wore a tiara with points on it that looked like quartz, and most interestingly—she wore cowboy boots and fairy wings.

"Here they are!" she practically yelled. She sounded a lot like Lizzie's mom. She rushed over to Olive and Peter and enveloped them in a hug. Olive wasn't quite sure where to put her hands— the fairy wings were in the way. In fact, one of them was almost in her mouth.

Before she could say anything, Aunt Willow let them go and waved them over to the table. "Come over here and sit down! We have some apple cider donuts to eat—we can't eat them all. Olive and Peter, tell me everything about yourselves, starting with when you were born."

Olive said, "What . . . ?"

Aunt Willow kept going. "Do you know the time of your birth? And *where* you were born? We can do a star chart for you." She paused and squinted slightly. "I'm going to guess you're Capricorn."

Olive's mouth hung open. She hadn't understood any of what Aunt Willow had said. Except that she and Peter were Capricorn. Whatever that meant.

"They are!" Lizzie said, beaming.

"We don't know our birth times, but we were born in Boston," Peter said. "We can get you our birth times later, probably."

"What's a star chart?" Olive asked.

"No matter!" said Aunt Willow. "I can always read your tarot cards. Or your palms. We'll have fun no matter what!"

Olive had seen tarot card readers and palm readers at a Renaissance festival one time. Her dad John had been more than a little skeptical, but her other dad had wanted to get readings for Peter and Olive. Peter had sided with David; Olive had sided with John. Which was how it normally went. Olive caught eyes with Peter and widened hers. Peter smiled and shrugged. Olive knew what that meant: "It may be a little nuts but it's probably fun."

"Okay," said Aunt Willow. "Let's get you plied with some donuts; let's throw some pillows on the floor in the den; we'll do some tarot readings and some palm readings; and then I want to hear about every single thing that's been happening around here. Sound good?"

Sarah smiled. "Oh, man, do we have some stories to tell you."

CHAPTER 11

A Whole Lot of Nonsense in a Tiara

Aunt Willow sat on the floor with them all in a circle. All the throw pillows lay scattered on the floor, and candles glowed around them. Olive thought that might be a fire hazard, but she didn't say anything. She pushed her glasses up and listened to what Aunt Willow was saying about Sarah.

"So, the cards say you are going to have an

amazing autumn—you're doing a lot of different things you haven't done before, right?" she asked.

Sarah nodded eagerly. "Oh, yeah! We got to put together a zombie hayride AND a haunted barn this year."

Aunt Willow smiled. "Yes! I heard about that."

It took all of Olive's willpower not to say, "Well then, it wasn't the cards that told you that!"

So far, Peter, Lizzie, and Sarah had had their cards and their palms read. Olive thought it was silly—Aunt Willow didn't say anything that wasn't obvious or that she hadn't heard from her own family.

"Okay, Olive, your turn!" Aunt Willow said

brightly. Olive considered this and was about to speak when Aunt Willow said, "Oooh. I see we have a skeptic in the bunch."

Peter, Lizzie, and Sarah all said, "Yep," at the same time. Olive really wished they'd quit doing that. At least doing it without her. Or about her.

Aunt Willow's eyes turned kind. "That must be hard, being the only one."

Olive shrugged. She felt tears spring to her eyes. Maybe Aunt Willow did know some things. . . .

But before Olive could sit down and get a reading, Sarah jumped in. "Olive is skeptical about something we wanted to talk to you about, Aunt Willow."

"Yes?" Aunt Willow raised one eyebrow.

"Well . . . we think there's a ghost haunting us," Sarah said.

And with that, Peter, Lizzie, and Sarah poured out the whole story of Verity Wentworth. Then they went into all the strange happenings since they'd heard about the story.

The whole time they were talking, Aunt Willow remained impassive. She nodded or said "Mm-hmm" but didn't seem to be totally buying it.

Olive was relieved. Maybe she'd finally have someone on her side.

When they were finally done with the story, Aunt Willow sat up straight and cleared her throat. "I'm so glad you told me all of this. Because I have to be honest . . ."

Olive smiled. FINALLY someone would be on her side.

". . . I have definitely felt an unsettled spirit around here. I believe one hundred percent that you are being haunted by the ghost of Verity Wentworth. I do know that she lived here. I can confirm that."

Lizzie, Sarah, and Peter all let out a breath that sounded like a sigh of relief. But anger welled up in Olive. Anger and frustration. It bubbled out of her until she couldn't keep it in anymore. She fell back into some pillows.

"I can't believe it," she said to the ceiling.

"We know you don't believe it, Olive, but . . . ," Lizzie started, but Olive sat up again.

"OF COURSE I DON'T BELIEVE IT!" she said. "It's not real. It's not true! Why do you insist on believing in these dumb things?" She turned to Aunt Willow. "And you're an adult! You're supposed to tell the truth!"

She stood up and stomped to her backpack. She unzipped it and grabbed a sheaf of papers. "I can prove it. Look at these things. These are the reasons all that stuff happened. I did some research."

She slammed the papers on the floor. "There. Look for yourself. The barn doors opened because there was a wind tunnel. And the pumpkin patch probably caught fire because of dumb kids smoking. And Sheriff Hadley is clumsy! EVERYTHING HAPPENED FOR A REASON. There is no such thing as ghosts!"

Olive thought everyone would grab the papers to thumb through them, but no one moved. They all just looked at her.

Aunt Willow cleared her throat. "Olive is right," she said, making Lizzie, Sarah, and Peter whip their heads around to stare at her. "There could be logical explanations for all of this." Olive smiled triumphantly. "BUT," Aunt Willow continued, "it wouldn't hurt to try to get Verity's ghost to move on. What do you say? Do you want some advice on how to do that?"

Lizzie, Sarah, and Peter all whooped. Olive fell back into the pillows again. "I'll be right back," Aunt Willow said. Then she sprang up and ran up the stairs. After just a few seconds, she came down again, holding a bag that had a moon and stars on it. "I have just the thing. I have a friend who is a medium, and I've gone on trips with her where we banished ghosts. I texted her and asked for some advice. Here's what I've got: a quartz crystal for clarity, rose quartz for love, a candle for burning, and tourmaline to banish negative energy. But also, ghosts sometimes just need justice. I think Gloria is right—you need to tell Verity Wentworth's story and find out who the real killer is."

"Did you have all of these things in your bag?" Sarah asked.

"Uh-huh!" Aunt Willow said cheerily. "I always carry these things around. For just this type of emergency, in fact." She smiled big. "Okay, kids. I need to go get some sleep. I have a heavy schedule of lucid dreaming tonight that I don't want to miss." She got up and gave each of them a hug.

As soon as she left, Sarah turned to Olive. "Okay, I'll say it. Olive, why are you being like this?"

CHAPTER 12
Clearing the Air

O live took a deep breath. "I just don't understand why you guys believe something that is ridiculous! Gloria was just trying to scare us—she thinks we're babies. You're falling right into her trap!" Now that she'd decided to talk about all her feelings, she couldn't seem to stop. "Why can't we just set up the zombie hayride and the haunted barn and just have fun? I'm right about ghosts not being real." She pushed her glasses up her nose. "Every single thing has a logical explanation. Why can't you see that?"

Two tears sprang to her eyes and then escaped. She wiped them away impatiently.

Lizzie said softly, "Why is it so important for you to be right about this?"

"Because . . ." Olive couldn't put it into words. "I don't know. It just seems that we're . . . not on the same page anymore. Or something."

Everyone was quiet. Olive knew they all felt the same way—this could be the beginning of the end. If she thought what they believed was baby-ish, how could they all come back from that? She felt like she was moving on and they were staying put, and it was not a good feeling.

Finally, Peter spoke. "Okay. So there IS

definitely a logical explanation for everything."

Olive looked at him in surprise. So did Lizzie and Sarah. He put his hands up. "I mean, the three of us aren't dumb, Olive. You may be the smartest person of all of us, but that doesn't mean we're not smart too."

Olive felt a zing of pride—her brother thought she was smarter than him? "I don't think I'm the smartest . . . ," she said, trailing off. But then she realized: she totally did. Because she totally was.

Peter went on, "But we keep saying this: you don't know everything. None of us do. Do you agree?"

Olive pursed her lips. She couldn't argue with that. "Yes, that's true."

"And the timing of all this stuff was really weird, right?" Peter continued.

"Yeah," she said slowly. "The timing was weird. But that's the thing about coincidences. They're weird."

Lizzie brightened up. She'd clearly seen where Peter was going. "But we don't know anything for sure, right? You just said that."

Olive nodded. "Yes, I guess not for SURE."

Peter finished up, "So, maybe we can agree that there are probably logical explanations for things. We all know that, Olive." Sarah and Lizzie nodded. "We agree with that. And all you have to do is agree to have an open mind."

Olive thought about it. She wasn't so sure. . . . They wanted her to have an open mind about something that couldn't be true. She *wanted* to have an open mind. "But . . . no one has ever seen a ghost for sure. Or proven they exist. It's hard to—"

Lizzie jumped in. "I've never seen gravity, but it exists."

Sarah's face brightened. "Yeah! I've never seen electricity, just the lightbulbs it goes into!"

Olive was about to argue that those things had been proven to exist, by lots of people and through all sorts of science, when Peter jumped in.

"I've never seen friendship walking around, but I know that exists," he said. He smiled at her.

That stopped Olive in her tracks. She saw Sarah smile widely, and Lizzie beamed. Olive's stomach untwisted. Her shoulders relaxed. A smile grew on her face, and it felt like it might hurt her cheeks if it grew any bigger.

"That's true!" she said. "Okay. I agree . . . I can do this." It felt like a huge weight had been lifted off her shoulders. She could keep her skepticism and be true to herself, and she could keep her friendship. The four of them threw their arms around each other and laughed. Olive felt better than she had in weeks.

Except for one thing . . .

"Okay, do you think Gloria was trying to scare us?" she asked them. "Or do you think she thinks the ghost is real?"

They broke out of their hug, and Lizzie looked thoughtful. She said, her voice hushed, "Knowing Gloria, it's probably both."

Peter nodded. "I think she was trying to scare us. Maybe to just get us in the mood for the haunted barn or something."

Sarah said, "Yep. That sounds like Gloria. Like she wanted us to get really into the story or something."

Olive said, "I bet she did some research or something. Anyway . . . what do you say we try to find out?"

Peter, Lizzie, and Sarah all looked at each other, and for a minute, Olive was afraid they were back to where they'd been before. She started to feel a little self-conscious, but then finally, the three of them broke out into huge grins.

"OH, YES," Sarah said. Then she lowered her voice. "And while we're at it, we can check for ghosts, too."

Olive beamed. "Deal," she said. Then she fell back into the pillows, glad the world was right again.

The next morning, all four of them got up early, ready to do some sleuthing on Gloria and her friends. Olive felt like they needed a plan, so she gathered them in closely at the breakfast table. They all kept one eye out for Gloria, but no one was too worried. She rarely got up before noon on weekends.

"Okay," Olive said. "It looks like we need to do two things. One, find out if Gloria is making that whole story up. Like, do she and her friends even believe it?"

Sarah chewed her toast and nodded. "Yeah, and if they don't believe it, she was just trying to be mean to us."

Lizzie said, "Or to practice storytelling. I don't think she would take the time to be mean unless it helped her acting."

Peter said, "Maybe to see if the story would

work on the people who came to the haunted barn."

Olive nodded, "Good, yes. So that's the first thing. That's going to be a lot of spying and following Gloria and her friends. Do you know what their schedule is like, Lizzie?"

Lizzie said, "They're practicing for the haunted barn today, I know that for sure. Gloria has told everyone that they're telling the story of Verity Wentworth to 'break the curse' and stop her from haunting the orchard. And 'WREAK-ING HAVOC' in the orchard. She always says that last part while she's throwing her arms out."

Olive giggled and pushed her glasses up. "Perfect. We can listen in on them and do a little spying to see if they all believe it or if Gloria was just making things up. But my idea for the second thing we can do is a little more . . . dangerous."

Lizzie, Sarah, and Peter all looked at her with puzzled expressions. Olive leaned in. "I think we should go to the barn at midnight with Aunt Willow's crystals and try to get the ghost of Verity Wentworth to leave the farm. Or to at least tell her that her story will be told."

Peter looked at her, disbelieving. "Wait. Miss Ghosts Aren't Real all of a sudden wants to talk to one?"

Olive grinned. "That's MS. Ghosts Aren't Real, thank you very much. And we agreed—we don't know everything, right? So we should try all avenues to get to the bottom of what's going on. Are you in?"

Sarah whooped and a piece of toast fell out of

her mouth. This made all four of them collapse in laughter. Peter managed to say, "It's the curse!" Which made them all laugh harder. Olive looked around at her friends and wondered how in the world she had ever felt like they didn't belong together.

CHAPTER 13
An Ill Wind

"You're on my foot, Olive!" Peter whispered loudly.

"Shhh," Sarah and Olive said at the same time, but that was so loud, all four of them ducked so they wouldn't be seen. They were sitting behind a bale of hay, watching Gloria and her acting friends rehearse for the Verity Wentworth grand finale in the haunted barn. Sneaking in and spying had been surprisingly easy. All they'd done was tiptoe into the barn one by one as the group of actors chatted in the hayloft and waited for rehearsal to start.

So far it just looked like a bunch of bored teenagers in black turtlenecks sitting around among the hay bales looking at their phones. But then Gloria clapped her hands and got everyone's attention.

When she spoke, she used a British accent that Olive had to admit was pretty good. "Daahllinnngs," she said, "thank you for coming to this wee little rehearsal. Your acting abilities are dangerously good, and we shall use your talent to make this the best haunted barn this world has ever seen!" She flung her arms out with a flourish, and the crowd of kids clapped wildly.

"First we'll do a few run-throughs. Then we'll

put on our makeup and do a dress rehearsal. The opening show is only two weeks away, my dears. We must get this perfect in order to wow our audience. Questions?"

It was quiet for a moment, and Olive heard rustling next to her. Lizzie had her hand over her nose, and her eyes had turned red and watery. She looked like she was going to sneeze. Olive shared a look with Sarah, who was scrunching up her face in anticipation, and the two of them nodded to each other. Then they dived on top of Lizzie just as she sneezed. The sound was muffled, but still, they weren't in the clear.

"What was that?" someone in the hayloft said. "Did you hear that?"

Gloria sniffed. "Darlings, our audience is not just the living. The dead come here tonight as well, to see our brilliance!" She flourished her hands again, but this time no one clapped.

"Gloria, we're not your little sister and her friends, you know. You don't need to try to scare us too," one of the turtlenecked actors said. Olive had poked her head up again when the person had mentioned them. This was exactly why they'd come to eavesdrop. Lizzie, Sarah, and Peter poked their heads up too.

"The story, dearest Jenny, is a true one. At least the part about Verity Wentworth being here and dying," Gloria said. Olive could see her glare from where she sat.

Another voice spoke out. "Yeah, but the other part—the murder and the ghost—was made up. Which was a pretty fabulous publicity stunt, Glor."

"Thank you, Natalie," Gloria said. "That was

a bit of genius on my part, I do admit. And my sister and her friends were the perfect first audience. They spread the word faster than even I expected."

"It would have been nice," another voice called out, "if your story involved more people parts. It's pretty funny how you get to play Verity Wentworth, and Pete gets to play Baron von Steuben, and the rest of us have to play farm animals."

"'Funny' is not the word, dear Meg. I believe the word 'genius' still applies. But we are wasting precious time! Let us all relive this story of Verity Wentworth!"

Peter looked at Lizzie, Sarah, and Olive and made a motion for them to get going. It was perfect timing because the actors had started grumbling and milling about, and many of them were whispering in twos. No one was paying attention to the ground floor of the barn, so the four of them snuck out. Without discussing it, they walked to the picnic table and sat down.

Olive could see the disappointed looks on her friends' faces. Sarah was the first one to speak: "So Gloria did make that all up." Lizzie traced a shape with her finger on the picnic table, and Peter looked out toward the creek.

It was funny how much difference a day could make. Even finding out she was right, Olive was miserable. Because her friends were.

She took a deep breath. "So . . . two things," she said. "Weird things have still been happening, right? I mean, Gloria likes attention, but even she doesn't want to ruin the orchard. So I really don't think she would start a fire or let the horses out. And I'm guessing she doesn't know anything about wiring lamps. So all that stuff . . . is still unexplained. And remember how Sheriff Hadley said it was weird that the hay was moved right where he fell? We definitely still need to figure out exactly what happened there. Even if it wasn't a ghost, there are still things to get to the bottom of!"

Peter, Lizzie, and Sarah nodded, but she could tell that the thought wasn't very cheery. She went on, "But the second thing . . . well, I think we could have a lot of fun if we did a prank on Gloria, the way she did a prank on us."

This perked everyone up. Sarah's eyes got round and excited and she said, "YES. That is a great idea!"

Lizzie nodded and squeaked a little, and Peter said, "Yeahhh." The mood at the table had lifted.

Olive smiled and pushed her glasses up. "Okay, so even Gloria thinks this is a made-up story. What if we pulled a prank that made it seem like it *wasn't* made up?"

"Perfect," Sarah said, but then got quiet.

After a second, Lizzie said, "How do we do that?"

Olive thought for a minute. "Can you record voices on your phone, Lizzie? Or Sarah?"

Lizzie nodded, but Sarah said, "My phone is so old it could be in Annabelle's Antiques."

Olive laughed. "Ours, too," she said. "All because our dads didn't want us playing games on the phone." Peter just shook his head.

Lizzie said, "It's only 'cause of my whole getting lost thing. This phone has GPS. And yeah, it also has a voice recorder thingy."

"And do you remember that your mom talked about speakers and stuff in the barn? So that we could play spooky music during the haunted barn, Sarah?" Olive asked.

Sarah said, "Oh, yeah! I do remember that."

Lizzie said, "I know they're set up! I heard my dad playing something really old out there the other night. Plus! Oh!" she said, bouncing on the picnic table bench. "This is perfect too, because my phone is connected to the speakers! My mom tried it out the other night and needed to use my phone." She squeaked, and Sarah high-fived her.

"Perfect! It's like this was meant to be," Olive said, even though she didn't believe in that sort of thing. "I think it's about time we show Gloria that she's not the only one with some great ideas around here."

CHAPTER 14

A Prank to Remember

Making the recording had been hilarious and hadn't taken them any time at all. With the voice recorder, it had been incredibly easy. Sneaking back into the barn proved to be harder. The actors had gotten bored and many of them hung around outside for a while, talking. Olive heard a lot of them complaining about the silly roles they were playing. She overheard one boy saying,

"I'm being wasted here! I'm more than a goat."

But finally, as the sun began to set, all four of them made it into the barn. It was close to dinnertime, and the light in the barn was beginning to dim. It was just eerie enough to give their prank an authentic boost. Gloria yelled, "That's a wrap!" and looked at her clipboard, taking her pen from behind her ear and making notes.

Behind the same bale of hay as before, Peter, Olive, and Sarah waited for the perfect moment to play the recording. Olive kept an eye out toward the doors, making sure no actors wandered in. Lizzie sat next to her phone, ready to hit the Play button. The speakers had been hidden right under the hayloft's floorboards, in the rafters, so the sound would be perfect for what they wanted to do.

Almost all of the actors had left, and it was

just Gloria and a few of her friends in the hayloft. Olive could hear Gloria saying, "Method acting!" and "LIVE INTO YOUR PARTS, DARLINGS." This made Olive roll her eyes, but the actors seemed to take Gloria very seriously. At some point, Olive wanted to investigate that strange phenomenon too.

When it was just Gloria and two other people in the hayloft, Olive knew it was time. They needed to play the prank on Gloria with witnesses. That would make everything seem that much more real.

Olive looked at Sarah, who nodded. Peter saw the look and nodded too. Lizzie glanced up, and all three of them nodded at her, their expressions serious. Lizzie pressed play.

"Gloooorrriiiiaaaaaa," the recording said softly.

Gloria snapped her head up. "Did you hear that?"

"Hear what?" one of the actors said.

"My name," said Gloria.

The actor looked around. "I don't think so." She looked at the other actor.

"I heard something," he said, but then he pointed to something in his hand. "Are you sure I should say this line, 'I must have you'? What if I said, 'As the crow flies, as the wind blows, as the sun must set in the east, I WILL have you'?"

Gloria fixed him with a stare—Olive could feel the ice from where she sat. "First, the sun sets in the west, my dear. Second, Baron von Steuben had no poetry in his heart! The line stays the same."

"Glooooooorrrriiiiiaaaaa," the recording said again. This time, Olive had to put her hand over her mouth to stop from laughing.

"There it is again!" Gloria said. "I know I heard it that time."

The actor who had just been scolded by Gloria said, "Not everything is about you, Gloria. You can't keep behaving like this. You'd better start listening to me . . ." He grabbed a bag and stood up straight. "Let's go, Lyra," he said to the other actor. "I'm sure my parents await us somewhere. If you want a ride, come with me."

Lyra shrugged at Gloria and grabbed her bag too. They made their way down the ladder of the hayloft and walked out the barn doors. Olive, Sarah, and Lizzie ducked down low so they wouldn't be seen. But as Olive watched the actors walk out, she realized there was no danger of that. The boy heatedly whispered to Lyra as they walked and didn't look up once.

This wasn't exactly what they'd planned— they'd hoped others would be there for the recording. But this was the next-best thing.

Olive motioned to Lizzie to up the volume on the phone just a little. She mimed "Play," and Lizzie once again hit the button.

"Gloooooooorrrrriiiiaaaaaaaaaa," the voice rang out again.

Now Gloria stood stock-still. She looked around, her eyes wide. Olive could see her swallowing hard, even in the dim light of the barn.

"Tellllll mmmmyyyy stooorrryyyyy," the recording said, and Olive had to stop herself from giggling again.

Suddenly, Gloria stood up tall. "I KNEW I was right, Verity. I knew it. I WILL tell your story. Mark my words! We shall avenge you!"

Now Olive, Peter, Sarah, and Lizzie all looked at each other. Gloria had thought she was telling a true story the whole time?

The recording said, "Tellllll myyyyy stoooooor-rrryyyy . . . . OR ELSE!"

Just as the last word came out, a wind picked up somewhere outside and blew the hay around. Something slammed on top of the hayloft, and the barn floor rattled.

Without looking at each other, all four of them crouched and ran out the barn doors. Olive could hear Gloria saying, "I hear you, Verity!" and when she looked back, she saw Gloria jumping out of the hayloft and sprinting out the other end of the barn.

But Olive didn't look long. Because nothing she knew could possibly have explained the sudden wind and the shaking barn. Or the sudden terrible feeling that they had not been alone.

CHAPTER 15
Stronger Together ... Right??

At the picnic table, the four friends caught their breath. With the sun down, the trees seemed to be looming over them. The wind picked up and scattered leaves, and Olive shivered. Suddenly, everything looked dangerous and dark.

"Um, can we go back to your house, Lizzie?" she asked.

Lizzie, white as a ghost, nodded. They walked

fast to the house, all three of them checking behind them just in case.

"What *was* that?" Sarah asked as they walked.

Olive shook her head. She had no words. She had no explanation.

Peter said, "That was . . . scary."

Lizzie squeaked.

Olive said, "I can't think of one logical reason that wind came up. Not one. Except, I guess, winds do happen . . . and it is fall. . . ." But her words trailed off. Even she didn't believe herself. She was right, of course. But that wind hadn't felt . . . right, somehow.

"Well, at least we know not to go into the barn again!" Peter said, laughing.

But Olive stopped in the path. "Actually, Peter, that's exactly what we'll be doing."

Lizzie and Sarah stopped too, and Peter's eyebrows rose. "What do you mean?"

Olive pushed up her glasses. "I'm still not convinced we're dealing with a ghost. But if that wind had something to do with anything ghostlike, then I think it's time for phase two of our plan." She squared her shoulders. "I think it's time to meet Verity Wentworth."

Peter groaned. "NOW you decide to embrace the idea of a ghost?"

Olive smiled. "Look, I don't know about you, but I'm pretty excited for the zombie hayride and the haunted barn. Well, the *fake* haunted barn, anyway. It's one of the first things that made us friends, right? I'm going to fight for that. I'm not about to let a two-hundred-year-old ghost ruin something we've been excited about for months.

Or try to get in the way of something so important to our friendship." She looked around and smiled at them, trying to look braver than she felt. "Besides— nothing can stop us if we're together, right?"

Her brother and her friends looked back at her and nodded.

Olive sincerely hoped she was right.

That Saturday night, a week before the haunted barn officially opened, the four of them put on black clothes, waited until midnight, and snuck out of Lizzie's house. They brought with them flashlights, crystals, a candle, and some words printed from the internet that Sarah had found.

Olive tried to gather her courage, but for some reason she found it hard to catch her breath. Even after they'd started on the path to the barn, with a huge full moon lighting the way, Olive felt like she was being watched. She did not like that feeling. Not only because it didn't make any sense, but also because . . . well, being watched at night felt SUPER-creepy. No one spoke as they walked, but Olive could see the ghostly breath puffing out of all of their mouths. It was usually brisk this time of year, but the weather was all over the place, so fog hung above the pumpkin patch and covered the ground as they neared the barn. The wind blew softly and made the leaves skitter across the grass and the gravel. The sound made Olive wince.

They got to the doors of the barn and looked at each other.

"Ready?" Olive asked, though she did not feel ready in the least.

"Ready," said Peter and Sarah. Lizzie squeaked.

They pushed the old barn doors, and the doors creaked open. The barn inside was half dark and inky, half lit by moonlight. Olive took a deep breath and stepped in.

It was like stepping into a freezer—somehow the air in the barn was colder than the air outside. Peter turned on his flashlight, and the rest of them got out theirs.

Sarah whispered, "Should we go to the hayloft?"

No one spoke, but they all walked to the ladder that led up to the hayloft. Peter went first, then Sarah, then Lizzie, then Olive. Olive had to stop herself from clambering up the ladder ahead of the others so she wouldn't be the last one climbing. When they got to the top, Lizzie cleared an area in the middle of the loft and sat down cross-legged. They all followed suit.

Sarah cleared her throat. "I guess, we light the candle?" she whispered. Olive wasn't sure why she was whispering, but she felt it was the right thing to do anyway.

Lizzie said, "Remember, we have to be really careful with the candle. We don't want another fire here." She mumbled, "My mom and dad would kill me if they knew I brought this in here. . . ." Then she swallowed and lit the candle, letting the smoke travel up. Aunt Willow had told them the smoke and their "intentions" would call Verity out to appear to them. Lizzie twirled the candle in the air and the light flickered off the walls. Then she whispered, "Now what?"

Olive cleared her throat. "Sarah, read the

words you found. Maybe that will do something."

Peter added, "Let's make sure the crystals are out too."

The four of them opened their palms to expose the crystals while Lizzie kept moving the candle in circles. The smoke from the wick seemed to intensify, and soon the hayloft was hazy. Sarah, not whispering anymore, started saying the words she'd found.

"Dear Name of Spirit," she started loudly.

Olive let out a nervous giggle, and Peter and Lizzie smiled. Olive said, "I think you're supposed to put the name of the ghost in there."

Sarah said, "Oh, yeah. Duh. Sorry. I'm nervous." Lizzie patted her shoulder and she went on. "Dear Verity Wentworth, we come to you today to ask you to go to the light. We have heard

your story. We know it needs to be told. Trust us and we will let the world know who wronged you. You are free."

Nothing happened.

Olive didn't know what she'd expected. Especially since she'd been skeptical from the beginning. But somehow, this was a letdown.

Sarah huffed out. "Well, that seemed pointless."

Peter sighed. "It was worth a shot."

Lizzie's shoulders slumped. "I can't help it; I'm a little disappointed," she said, looking at the others.

But right at that moment, the candle blew out. And all their flashlights shut off on their own.

CHAPTER 16
Those Meddling Kids

O live, Peter, Lizzie, and Sarah all screamed
at the same time. The barn had turned
pitch black—even the moonlight didn't
seem to be streaming in anymore. Olive stood up
to hurry down the ladder but smacked right into
Peter. Who smacked into Lizzie. Who smacked
into Sarah. All four of them went down in a heap.

Then the light changed. Something seemed
to glow outside the barn doors. As Olive watched

in fear and fascination, a ghostly figure floated into the barn. It was a small woman dressed in clothes that looked like they were from long-ago colonial days. The woman seemed to be mouthing something and looking into the distance.

At the same time, a breeze came from nowhere and ruffled Olive's hair, and a sound like a low moaning floated through the barn.

Olive couldn't move. She had never before in her life seen anything so scary. This seemed so real. The real Verity Wentworth—or her ghost, anyway—was actually haunting the orchard.

She had been wrong, clearly. Totally, 100 percent wrong.

The already-cold temperature in the barn dropped even lower, and now Olive could see her breath. She looked over at Lizzie, Sarah, and

Peter and could see their breath too. When she looked down, she even saw the ghost's breath.

Olive grabbed Peter's hand and huddled close. She gathered up her courage and said, "Verity Wentworth. We know it is you. We WILL tell your story!" She felt Lizzie and Sarah and Peter all crowd against her. They would protect each other, Olive knew this for sure. Something rattled in the back of her mind, but before she could figure out what it was, the ghost spoke.

"It is tooooooo late," the woman said, still looking off into the distance. "You didn't believe . . . no one believes." Then the woman turned suddenly to the four in the hayloft. She looked up and pointed at them. "YOU DIDN'T BELIEVE!" Her face turned into a mask of fury, and her breath came in uneven gasps. Olive felt her whole body stiffen in fear, and then . . . and then the thing rattling at the back of her mind came into focus.

The ghost's breath.

Ghosts don't breathe.

Olive snorted a little. Then she snorted a lot. Then she began hysterically laughing. Gloria and her friends had almost gotten them. Olive had to admit they were good. Sarah, Lizzie, and Peter stared at her like she'd lost her mind. That only made her giggle more. The "ghost" below even had a confused look on her face.

Finally, Olive got herself together and said, "All right, Gloria, that was pretty good. But you can come out now."

The woman below the hayloft yelled, "There is no Gloria!"

But Olive stood tall and put her hands on

her hips. "Oh, yeah? Okay, *ghost,* tell me why it is you're breathing? I thought you were dead." She felt Lizzie, Peter, and Sarah stand up straight beside her. She heard their giggles now too.

The woman below sputtered, "Th-this is but a phantom . . . it's phantom breath! I . . . You have no idea . . ." Then the woman just stopped. "Ah, well. You got us. Gloria, they figured it out," she said. She reached up and took off her wig. She reached under her skirts and took out a few lights and a flashlight, and other people came into the barn with flashlights too.

Now that Olive had a better look, she could see that the ghost wasn't a small woman at all, but one of Gloria's friends whom she'd seen at the rehearsal the other night.

Gloria swept in. "Pretty good for *babies,*" she

said, throwing her scarf around her shoulder. Looking at her friend, she said, "You couldn't have held your breath?"

Her friend scoffed and said, "It's way too cold in here. And anyway, we should run lines for the set we'll be performing. We don't have much time, and all this goofing around isn't helping." She waved her arms. "Come on, guys. Let's go back to the house and start over. Now that the script actually includes more lines for actors and we're not all barn animals anymore, we need to practice." More people in black appeared by the girl, all holding flashlights. One of them also held a phone. He pressed a button and the low moaning sound stopped. Olive knew exactly where the sound came from—small speakers underneath the hayloft.

Looking up at the hayloft, the girl who'd played Verity Wentworth said, "Good job, kids. Keep a skeptical eye out. But be sure to catch our performance when the haunted barn actually opens up. We're pretty good. You coming, Gloria?"

Gloria said, "In a minute." Everyone on the ground floor left except Gloria. Olive, Peter, Lizzie, and Sarah looked at each other. They grabbed their flashlights and turned them on again. Then they made their way down the ladder to talk to Gloria.

When they reached the ground, Olive said, "So you figured out we'd tricked you?"

Gloria smiled a smug smile. "One cannot fool a fooler, babies. I act for a living. I know staging when I see it. Or hear it."

Lizzie said, "Gloria, where did you get that story about Verity?"

Gloria shrugged. "Oh, Aunt Willow had a dream. And I *may* have embellished it a little. But you have to admit—it's got DRAMA! Why, were you scared?" She put her flashlight under her chin to make her face look scary.

Olive said truthfully, "I wasn't. At least not until tonight."

Gloria shrugged and put the flashlight down. "Well, three out of four babies will do." She turned to leave, but Olive said, "Wait."

She pushed her glasses up on her nose and tried to organize her thoughts. She still wasn't quite sure how Gloria had done everything.

"Okay, so we know you used the speakers under the hayloft like we did," Olive said.

Gloria barked a laugh. "Yes! I was there when they installed them. As if I wouldn't know where the sound the other night was coming from . . ."

"And we know that your friend put lights under her skirt so it looked like she was glowing. How did you make it look like she was floating?" Olive asked.

"Oh, that's easy. She just wore black shoes and socks. And Jenny is an accomplished stealth walker. From your angle, it would look like she was floating."

Peter added, "And you used your flashlights to make the glow seem like it came from somewhere else, right?"

Gloria looked down her nose at Peter. "Every actor knows that lighting is everything."

Olive shook her head. "Okay, but how did you

make it so cold in here? And how did you shut off our flashlights? I mean, I know you just made a wind blow to snuff out the candle. But I can't figure out the other two things."

Gloria had gone still and stared at Olive. "Your flashlights went off?"

Olive said, "Nice try. How did you do it? Are these trick flashlights or something?"

Gloria shook her head slowly and backed up a little. Her voice had changed. It somehow sounded younger. "Um, we didn't do anything to make it this cold. In fact . . . has it gotten colder in here?"

Lizzie said, "It's over, Gloria. Just tell us how you did it. Or I'll tell Mom and Dad that you tried to scare us."

Gloria glared at Lizzie. "Well, I'll tell Mom

and Dad that you were out of the house in the middle of the night."

Peter said, "But wait, are you really saying you don't know how the flashlights got turned off?"

Sarah said, "Maybe they just malfunctioned?"

Right at that moment, the flashlights that Olive, Peter, Sarah, Lizzie, and Gloria held all shut off again. And then the barn doors shut with a BANG, leaving them in total darkness.

CHAPTER 17

Illuminating the Issue

All five of them screamed and ran for the doors. Peter reached them first and yanked on them, but they wouldn't budge. The rest of the group rushed to help, but none of them could get the doors open.

A low light emanated from behind them. Olive whispered, "Gloria, are your friends still messing with us?"

Olive could see Gloria's eyes, wide and afraid.

She'd never seen Gloria like this since she'd known her. She'd always seemed world-weary and like nothing would surprise her. But this expression . . . Gloria looked as terrified as Olive felt.

Gloria whispered back, "I don't think this is them."

All five of them turned around slowly.

The light seemed to have no form—it was just a glowing ball. The cold was back, this time so frigid that Olive started shaking, though she wasn't sure if that was from the cold or from the fact that they might be staring at a ghost.

"Wh-wh-what do you want?" Sarah asked.

The glowing ball of light just sat there.

"Are you going to hurt us?" Peter asked it.

The light dimmed.

"Do you want to tell us something?" Gloria asked. The light grew brighter, then went back to the way it had been before. Now Olive thought she got it.

"Am I Olive Wu?" Olive asked. Sarah, Lizzie, Peter, and Gloria looked at her. She whispered, "I think it's dimming for no and growing brighter for yes. So I'm doing a test."

The light grew brighter, then went back to normal. "Are we on planet Earth?" Olive asked it. The light grew brighter again.

"Is Gloria an alien?" Lizzie asked. The light dimmed.

Gloria stared at Lizzie and she shrugged. "It said no," she grumbled.

Olive swallowed. "Are you Verity Wentworth?"

Nothing happened for a moment, and then

the light grew brighter and then resumed its normal state.

A shudder ran through the group. Sarah asked, "What do you want us to do?" But Peter whispered, "You have to ask it yes-or-no questions!"

Sarah said, "Oh, yeah. I forgot. Okay, are you here to hurt us?"

The light dimmed. Olive relaxed just a little, but not totally. Because if a vengeful spirit wanted to hurt them, it would also probably lie to them.

On top of that, they were talking to a ball of light. Nothing made sense to Olive at the moment.

Gloria stepped up. "Was my aunt Willow right about your story? Were you killed by Baron von Steuben?"

As before, there was a beat, but then the light

grew so bright, all five of them had to cover their eyes. It finally dimmed back to its normal glow.

Olive swallowed. "If we tell your story, will that help you be free?"

The light brightened again.

Gloria squared her shoulders. "Then we will tell your story exactly as it should be told. Starting next weekend—everyone will know what happened to you!"

Lizzie said, her voice small, "We're so sorry that happened to you."

The ball of light grew brighter and brighter until everyone hid their eyes again. Then, with a flash, the light was gone. All of their flashlights turned on again, and the barn doors swung wide open. The barn also seemed to warm up.

Olive was the first to speak. "That was . . ."

Sarah said, "CREEPY!" They all nodded.

Olive turned to Gloria. "Tell us the truth, were your friends playing a prank on us? Do you know?"

Gloria looked serious. She said, "If they were, that was a really cool trick. I guess they could have made that light. Maybe these are trick flashlights. . . ."

But then Olive finished the thought. "But we still don't know how they could have made it so cold. . . ."

No one spoke.

"Well," Peter said. "Whoever or whatever it was, we know we need to tell the story, at least."

Gloria stood up tall. "Indeed we do. Next week, ACTING will save lives!" She threw her scarf around her shoulders again, and her usual

Gloria expression came back. Here was the Gloria Olive knew. "I need to go practice my art, babies. If I were you, I'd try to find a way to help us tell the story."

With that, Gloria swept out of the barn and into the night.

CHAPTER 18

Superspies

Lizzie, Sarah, Peter, and Olive practically ran back to Lizzie's house. When they got there, the house somehow seemed big and shadowy. The full moon illuminated the fog traveling behind the house. Even the snorting of the horses all the way from the barn put Olive on edge.

Once inside, they piled all their pillows and

sleeping bags together in the family room and huddled up in the middle of the floor. No one said anything for a minute.

Lizzie said quietly, "I thought I'd be kind of excited about a ghost, but I don't know if I am anymore."

Olive felt Peter shiver next to her, and she snuggled closer. She was scrunched between him and Lizzie, but she didn't mind at all.

Sarah said, "I just don't know if I believe Gloria . . . That had to be a prank, right?"

Olive thought for a minute. "I don't know how. I really don't."

Peter said, "That plus the other things . . . the horses being let out. The pumpkin patch fire. The lightbulb exploding . . ."

Lizzie said, "Olive, can you think of reasons all of that happened? I mean, besides a ghost?"

The question made Olive warm and happy. Why had she ever thought her friends didn't listen to her? She thought about it for a very long time. She heard Sarah start to snore just a little bit when she finally started talking again. "Well, with the weird stuff that happened before, there are reasonable explanations. Everyone getting hurt in the barn really could just be because there was a lot of activity and people are clumsy. Especially Sheriff Hadley," she said, looking over at Sarah.

Sarah snorted. "That's for sure. Good thing my mom is his good friend—he always needs help with something."

Olive said, "Just frie—I mean, yep. That's

true." Peter elbowed her and smiled. She smiled back. "And like the research I found says, the barn doors could have been opened by a wind tunnel," she continued. "And the lightbulb exploding really could have been an old house thing. I read about other old houses having weird electricity problems."

Peter said, "Maybe they had ghosts, too."

Olive thought about that for a moment. "Huh. I never thought about it that way. Anyway, as far as the pumpkin patch goes, I don't really have an answer for that."

Lizzie spoke up. "You mentioned that it could have been kids. That is really true. Some kids like to hang out around the patch some-times. And I think some of them"—she lowered her voice—"smoke."

"Hmm, yeah," Olive said. "If they didn't put their cigarette out right, it could have started a fire."

"Gross," Peter said. They all nodded.

"Okay, so that's all the stuff we kind of knew about anyway. What about tonight?" Sarah asked.

"Here's where I'm stuck. So, I think the light tonight could have been made. Maybe one of the actors had some remote-controlled thing? They could have kept the barn doors shut. But the cold . . . and the flashlights going off . . . I don't know how they'd do that," Olive said.

"Did we ever check the flashlights?" Sarah suddenly asked.

No one answered.

Olive sighed. "I don't think we're done with spying tonight, you guys," she said.

All three of them sat up on their elbows and looked at her. She sat up too. "I think we need to check Gloria's room to see if she has anything that could make all that stuff happen tonight."

Peter said, "I don't know, Olive. She seemed really scared."

But Lizzie looked thoughtful. "Well, maybe. But she is actually a really good actor. I've heard other people say it—she takes it seriously and she's amazing at it. She could have been acting."

Olive stood up and stepped over the wall of pillows. They were all still in their black clothes—no one had wanted to get into pj's.

"Who's up for looking in Gloria's room?" she asked. No one said anything. "Yeah, me neither. But let's go."

Everyone got up off the floor.

Olive put her hand on the doorknob and Lizzie turned on the flashlight on her phone, pointing it toward the floor. Olive looked back at the others, and they all gave her a nod. She turned the doorknob and tiptoed into Gloria's room, the others following her.

The place was super-clean, which was somehow surprising to Olive. She'd expected it to be strewn about with feather boas and sunglasses. Instead, there were a bed, a dressing table, a dresser, and a desk. And big windows that let in all the moonlight. Gloria lay in her bed, an eye mask over her eyes. She was snoring softly.

Peter motioned to a corner of the room. A big knapsack sat in the corner. It was the only thing out of place in the whole room. Olive nodded.

She tiptoed forward and the floor made a loud CREAK. Olive froze. So did the rest of them. Gloria sat straight up in bed, the mask still over her eyes. She muttered something that sounded to Olive like "staniskofbee." But then she fell back into bed and resumed snoring.

The four of them snuck over to the bag and opened it. Lizzie trained her light inside.

Sure enough, a remote control sat in there.

"That must have been for the flashlights," Olive whispered.

There was also a round ball that had lights attached to it and a translucent string attached to its top.

Lizzie sat back on her heels. "The glowing light," she whispered.

Peter said softly, "There must have been others in the barn who helped make it seem like it was floating and answering our questions."

Olive felt around in the bag and only came up with a clipboard and a pen and various small props. None of it was anything that had appeared in the barn.

They snuck back out of the room and

reconvened in their blankets and pillows. Lizzie yawned big.

Olive said, "So we know how they did the glowing ball. And our flashlights, but . . ."

Sarah finished, "How'd they make it so cold in there? Lizzie, is the electricity installed yet?"

Lizzie shook her head. "No, they're doing that tomorrow."

"We would have heard anything that needed electricity. A generator would have been really loud," Peter said.

Olive let out a long breath. "Well, because I don't know everything, and I've kept an open mind, the logical conclusion is . . . we may just have a ghost on our hands. So what do we do next?" She looked at all of them and saw their giant smiles, and she had to smile back too.

"Let's call Aunt Willow tomorrow," Lizzie said. "We'll tell her the ritual didn't work and get her advice. Then we can solve this once and for all."

CHAPTER 19
The Play's the Thing

Olive couldn't believe it—the time for the zombie hayride and the haunted barn had finally come. She looked at her friends, who were dressed in different zombie costumes, and smiled.

"Remember when we first met and found out we all loved zombies?" Olive said.

Sarah grinned. "Yeah, I wasn't very nice to you then. But you and Peter kinda grew on me."

Peter smiled at her, and Lizzie squeaked. Olive smiled too. "Clearly, I've always liked to be right," she said. "But I was definitely right about you guys."

Before anyone could respond, Ms. Shirvani came up with Sheriff Hadley, who was dressed as a zombie too. She had her arm through his and she looked thrilled. "Hey, honey!" she said to Sarah. Then she asked everyone, "Are you all ready for the first customers? Tell me how this goes again?"

Lizzie said, excited, "It goes like this! The people go on the hayride and get to shoot zombies with Nerf guns."

Sarah narrowed her eyes. "Aren't you a zombie to shoot at?" she asked Sheriff Hadley.

He grinned. "Nope. I'm the law around these

here parts. Tonight I'm just the zombie law." He winked, but Sarah looked at him suspiciously. Something in her face said she noticed her mom's arm through his . . . and wasn't quite sure about it.

Lizzie jumped in. "So then the customers get off the hay wagon and hand off their Nerf guns. Then we get to chase them into the barn! They go through all the rooms and end in the big open area, where Gloria and her friends tell the story of Verity Wentworth."

Which, Olive thought, *could get rid of a ghost if it existed . . .*

But then a commotion rippled through everyone standing around the haunted barn and interrupted Lizzie. The hay wagon had been spotted! Albert Garrison cheerily drove the wagon with the first hayride customers, and a zing of excitement shot through Olive. Sarah clapped her hands, Lizzie squeaked, and Peter laughed. Olive said, "YES!" and shared gleeful smiles with the rest of them. They ran to take their places outside the barn, along with a few other zombies.

"Do you have the powder?" Peter whispered to Olive. She nodded and patted her pocket.

She gave a thumbs-up to all three of them, and they squatted down behind the barn to wait for the people they would chase inside.

The powder in Olive's pocket was a whole bunch of herbs and spices they'd gathered from the Garrisons' spice cupboard and combined. Plus some dirt from the orchard field and ground hay from the barn. Aunt Willow had said it was "justice powder"—something much stronger than just the words and the crystals they'd tried to use the week before. Olive was doubtful, but she'd decided to trust Aunt Willow. Who knew? Just maybe Aunt Willow knew what she was talking about. Olive was keeping an open mind.

The first happy screams from the customers reached their ears, and they saw the customers jump off the hay wagon and run toward the barn. Tabitha Garrison stood outside, yelling, "This way to escape the zombies! This way!" And then she made the signal for the next wave of zombies to chase the customers into the barn. Olive was already giggling, but in seconds they were running and limping and dragging their feet toward the customers. Peter made a long moaning sound, and Sarah groaned too. Lizzie limped and giggled, and Olive put on her best spacey look and shuffled toward the customers running into the barn.

The customers ran inside, screaming the whole way, and the four zombie friends followed. They ran partway down the first aisle in the barn and then ducked under some long curtains that separated the rooms. They ended up in the area around the hayloft—exactly where they were supposed to be.

Gloria and her friends mingled up above in the loft, and some of them muttered to themselves, clearly practicing lines. Olive heard the screams of the first wave of customers going through the barn, hitting all the rooms. She smiled to herself—this really was the coolest thing to be a part of. She could hear Hakeem roaring and knew he was operating the chainsaw (without the chain) and scaring the customers. She could hear Stella cackling over the dentist chair. She heard Aaron and Faiyaz, and even Dani, doing their parts to scare everyone. The town had come together to help out the Garrison Orchard. Just like they'd done for Verity Wentworth. Well, not exactly the same, but close.

Suddenly, it was time for the play. Customers spilled out of the last room and huddled together, looking excited and scared, almost below the hayloft, staring up at the lights. Lizzie, Sarah, Peter, and Olive tiptoed around so that they were under the hayloft but could still see up. It was so dark in the barn, except where the actors were, that Olive wasn't worried that they would distract the customers.

Gloria appeared as Verity Wentworth and spoke. "I am but a simple farmer who loves the land. My family wishes to stay here and prosper. But then Papa had his accident—we are in serious trouble. I try and try to work this land, but it is too much without Papa. I am running out of options." Then Gloria broke into tears.

An actor spoke next, his voice filled with malice. "Verity Wentworth, I have heard about your plight. My name is Baron von Steuben and I have seen you in town. I want you as my wife. I will think about saving your paltry farm . . . but we must marry first. These are my terms to save your land and your family."

Gloria said, "But I shall not marry you, sir! And to demand that I do in such a way shows that you are no gentleman!" The emotion in Gloria's voice gave Olive goose bumps, and she heard Lizzie gasp.

Other actors came in, carrying props. "Miss Wentworth, don't you worry," said one of the actors. "This town will help you. We wouldn't let you suffer. We take care of each other here." They handed her baskets of food, and many of the other actors at the side of the hayloft took hoes and rakes and pretended to work the land.

"How dare you!" the actor playing Baron von Steuben yelled.

Verity said, "I think you should get off my land, sir."

Baron von Steuben let out an infuriated howl and stomped off. The lights in the hayloft went off once but then came back on.

Verity sat in the middle, a spotlight just on

her. "I fear the evil man has sabotaged the farm. We awoke to fire and chaos, and our hard work has been undone. I will appeal to him and ask him to stop his rampage."

People in the audience below the loft murmured "No!" and Olive smiled. She'd felt the same way during the story.

Baron von Steuben joined Verity in the spotlight. "I see you've changed your mind," he said, laughing evilly.

Olive looked at the rest of her friends. It was almost time for them to do what they needed to do. Aunt Willow had given them specific instructions. When Gloria took her fall out of the hayloft, they would throw the powder in the air. Then they'd grab each other's hands and say some words together that they'd practiced almost all day long. They all seemed ready. Olive put her hand in her pocket and felt the powder, clenching her fist around it and getting ready to throw.

"I will NEVER marry you," Verity said. "I've asked you here to appeal to your humanity!"

"Never, eh? You'll never marry me? Well then, what good are you to me?" Baron von Steuben screamed. He took Verity by the shoulders and threw her.

Time seemed to stand still. Then three things happened at the same moment. A small glowing light appeared right where Gloria began to fall. The temperature in the barn dropped so that Olive could see her breath again. And a wind came out of nowhere, whipping people's hair around and making a low, keening sound through the whole place.

Then time sped up. Gloria dropped through the air and landed on the hay. Olive yelled "NOW!" and stepped in front of the people gathered in the middle of the room, now holding on to each other and looking genuinely scared. She threw the powder in the air over the glowing ball. For a moment, the powder seemed to settle around what appeared to be the shape of a woman. Olive's brother and their two best friends rushed to her side. They grabbed her hands, and together the four of them yelled, "Justice is served; your story's been told; the curse is over; peace be with you!"

The glowing ball grew brighter and brighter, as it had before, and then flashed and disappeared. But in that one flash, Olive swore she could see Verity Wentworth smiling at them.

And then the cold, the wind, the moaning, and the light disappeared completely.

CHAPTER 20
The Curse Is Lifted

Olive finished taking her makeup off in the bathroom and looked at the black-, red-, green-, and white-stained towel. She laughed—being a zombie sure was messy.

She walked back into the Garrisons' dining room, where her dads, the Garrisons, Ms. Shirvani, and the sheriff all sat, not to mention her twin brother and her two favorite friends in the world. Many of New Amity's citizens milled around the house, some of them still in costume from the haunted barn, all laughing and drinking hot apple cider. The house was cozy and bright, and Olive felt content. Their first night running the zombie hayride and the haunted barn had been an overwhelming success. And more than a few people had congratulated the Garrisons on the frightful performance.

Olive was on her way to sit down next to her brother when she saw Gloria in the hallway. Gloria beckoned to Olive and gestured for her to gather Lizzie, Sarah, and Peter, too. So Olive said, "Hey, Gloria wants to talk to us."

The four of them followed Gloria out the back door and to the gazebo, which was covered in orange and purple lights. The moon was bright, even though it wasn't full anymore, and though the air was chilly, it was a not-unpleasant change from the warm house. Gloria sat down on a bench in the gazebo and threw her scarf over her shoulder. Olive, Lizzie, Sarah, and Peter took seats too.

"Babies," Gloria started. "It seems we have been tricking each other. But now I ask for a truce. I will tell you my part if you tell me yours, regarding the events of the haunted barn."

Olive crossed her arms over her chest. "Why should we believe you? You lied before, clearly."

Gloria dropped the tone she normally used to speak to them. She spoke to them like she would to her friends. "Yes, that's true. All I can do is promise I'll tell the truth."

"Okay, you first," Sarah said, and Lizzie squeaked in agreement.

Gloria said, "We tricked you with that ball

of light. It was something we were workshopping for the show. And I did have flashlight remotes—Lyra found this cool new tool that you can put in flashlights to make them seem haunted. It's amazing what you can find at Halloween superstores."

Peter said, "Yeah, we knew that."

Gloria raised an eyebrow. "Oh? Methinks you've been somewhere you shouldn't have been, perhaps."

"What about the cold?" Olive asked.

Gloria got serious again. "I don't know. I didn't do that."

"The barn doors being shut?" Lizzie asked.

"Yes, that was us. But we didn't do any wind."

Olive asked, "How about the ball of light tonight? How'd you do it again with all those people there?"

Gloria breathed out. "Well, that's the thing . . . I cut the light from the show. Too distracting, I thought. And my friends swear they didn't do it. I mean, maybe they were mad 'cause I also cut some parts. But they're loyal to the craft! I don't think they would interrupt a performance."

Olive thought Gloria was telling the truth. Gloria went on, "So where did it come from?"

They all shifted uneasily. Lizzie said, "Did you all . . . did you all see the outline of someone? And then a flash of . . ."

Everyone in the gazebo answered, "Verity Wentworth," at the same time. Olive shivered.

"You said your aunt Willow had a dream about the Verity story?" Olive asked.

Gloria nodded.

"Well . . . Aunt Willow is the one who gave us

the recipe for the justice powder. Do you think, maybe . . ." Olive trailed off, not wanting to be the one to say it.

Peter looked at her. "So, do you believe we just saw a ghost?" he asked.

Olive took a deep breath. "Well, I know I don't know everything. And I believe that no matter what, we did something good tonight. I mean, we put on a spectacular hayride and haunted barn, right?" She grinned.

"You're okay with not knowing for sure?" Sarah asked.

"Yep. I know what I need to know right now—and that's that I have the best brother and the best friends in the world. And I live in the best town in the world. And, if I do say so myself, I make the best zombie in the world."

"Whatever!" said Sarah. "My zombie face was WAY better!"

Peter said, "Come on, my moan worked the best."

And even Lizzie said, "Sorry, guys, but I'm pretty sure my walk made me the scariest zombie."

Pretty soon they were all talking over each other and laughing, knocking into each other in mock indignation.

Gloria huffed out. "Such babies," she said, and stood up. She walked away, but then she turned around and winked at them.

Lizzie, Sarah, Peter, and Olive all winked back at her. And then continued arguing over who had made the best zombie ever.

ACKNOWLEDGMENTS

First and foremost, I have to thank my delightful, brilliant, and kind editor, Emma Sector, for her thorough reads, her enthusiasm, and her tactful and amazing edits! Honestly, everyone should get the chance to work with someone like Emma. She makes the whole editing process fun while still being a genius editor.

As always, a huge thank-you to my agent, Ammi-Joan Paquette, for her support and for sending me on the path for this series. Joan is simply awesome, and I'm always grateful and humbled to be represented by such a fantastic human being!

ACKNOWLEDGMENTS

Forever and always, I thank my friend-family: Anne, Jordan, Megan, Brett, Pete, Jenny, Natalie, and Patrick. And my other friend-family, which includes Sharon, Ella, Sophie, Shaun, and Sarah.

And, of course, a huge thank-you to my family-family: my parents, Scott, Brianna, Colette, and Melanie.

Finally, a BIG, BIG thank-you to you, dear reader. You make this all so much fun! Keep reading—it changes the world.

MEGAN ATWOOD is an author and an assistant professor at Rowan University whose most recent books include the Dear Molly, Dear Olive series. When she's not writing books for kids of all ages, she's making new friends, going on zombie hayrides, and visiting haunted houses. And, always, petting her two adorable cats, who "help" her write every book.

Don't miss Book 4:

A SPRING TO REMEMBER

The Orchard crew is trying their hand at matchmaking, but Lizzie isn't so sure the couple actually wants their help. Find out what happens in the fourth Orchard Novel!